THE CRISTA  CHRONICLES

THE SECRET OF
Moonlight
Mountain

Mark Littleton

HARVEST HOUSE PUBLISHERS
EUGENE, OREGON 97402

To Nicole

When you can read it,
I hope you enjoy it.

Secrets of Moonlight Mountain

Copyright © 1992 by Mark Littleton
Published by Harvest House Publishers
Eugene, Oregon 97402

Library of Congress Cataloging-in-Publication Data

Littleton, Mark R., 1950–
    Secrets of Moonlight Mountain / Mark Littleton.
        p.   cm. — (Crista chronicles series ; bk. 1)
    Summary: After her mother's death, twelve-year-old Cri-
sta can't seem to please her father, but she finds some
comfort in her artwork and with a teenage couple and two
dogs she discovers living in the nearby woods.
    ISBN 0-89081-960-2
    [1. Fathers   and   daughters—Fiction.   2. Artists—
Fiction.   3. Dogs—Fiction.   4. Christian   life—
Fiction.]   I. Title.   II. Series: LIttleton, Mark R.,
1950–   Crista chronicles series ; bk. 1.
PZ7.L7364Se   1992
[Fic]—dc20   92-3145
                                                                      CIP
                                                                       AC

Contents

· 1 ·

Major Mistake

Crista Mayfield and her father stared at the sunken rowboat. The motor end was deep in the water. The bow poked out of the water just a foot.

"Daddy, are you mad?"

There was a long, tired sigh. "No."

"Daddy, please tell me? Are you mad at me?"

"No, Crista. Let's just get it back out. I'll get Uncle Josh to help me pull it out." Uncle Josh was a neighbor, not really an uncle. But Crista called him Uncle and so did her father because he was very old and a good friend.

As Uncle Josh and Crista's father worked on the boat, Crista offered several times to help, but her father simply said, "It's too heavy and you'll slip and hurt yourself."

Afterward the two men talked on the beach. Crista listened for some sign of her father's mood, but as always she couldn't tell. She was sure he was angry with her, but he would never admit it. He rarely admitted anything. In fact, he hardly said a word—not since the accident when her mother had died.

"Have to clean that motor up good," Uncle Josh said.

"Yeah, it'll give me something to do in the basement this winter," her father answered.

Crista felt as if she weren't even there. When they finally finished, her father didn't even ask her to cover the boat properly. He did it himself.

Surges of anger catching her throat, Crista suddenly left and went back up to the house. She grabbed her backpack with her charcoals and drawing paper in it and ran out the front door. She knew her father wouldn't say any more about it, or even give her a chance to ask questions. The only place to go was the woods and the mountain. She hoped the stillness of the forest would calm her spirit and maybe give her an idea about what to do to make things right.

Half an hour later Crista tilted her face into the sunlight and closed her eyes. She let the warmth sift across her face. Perched on Elbow Rock, the troubles of home and her father's silences suddenly seemed far away. Her tears were already dried and she knew the pain would soon vanish. Deep down she realized he was still going through a bad time.

But she also knew she had to do something about it. Make him feel again. Make him love her again.

For a moment it made her smile the way he had taught her to cover the boat over two years ago. It was one of the few chores she had actually looked forward to doing. Instantly the scene jumped into her mind's eye as the sunlight kneaded with little jets of heat into her cheeks.

You button it down over the motor first," he said as she watched from the dock ramp. He bent over the motor fumbling with the strings. His bottom bobbed back and forth in the air and she laughed. When he turned around, she was grinning.

"What's so funny now? This is serious, Crista."

"I know. But your bottom." She giggled again.

He rolled his eyes and sighed with exasperation. "I suppose you're going to draw that, too!"

"Maybe!" Crista suddenly said, thinking it would be funny. Even the great Dutch artist Rembrandt would never have thought of such a thing!

As the memory faded, she discovered a hard lump throbbing in her throat. She hadn't realized how much she wanted her dad to be like that again.

Then suddenly she knew she had to draw it. She tugged out the pad of paper in her blue backpack now lying on the rock and quickly selected a thin charcoal pencil for a line drawing. Picturing the scene in her mind again, she began sketching the boat, motor, cover, and finally her father, his behind high up in the air and his face looking at her under his arm somewhat like a bird veiling its face with a wing.

The strokes came quickly. She was always quick in her drawing. Rarely did repeated etchings and erasings work for her. If she didn't get it the first time, she threw away the sheet of paper and started over. She learned long ago that erasures only made it worse. And that was one thing her father had never minded: He always bought her all the art supplies she asked for.

As the sunlight washed over the stark lines on the crisp white sheet, she smiled. It was her dad all right. She had even remembered the rip on his sleeve. Chuckling over the drawing, she told herself she would make him a good dinner tonight and maybe he would talk about the boat. Maybe he would even talk about something else, like he used to—before the accident when her mother was killed in town by a drunk driver.

She closed the notebook over the drawing and placed it gently back into her pack, then leaned back and inhaled deeply. As she did, she thought about prayer and how her mother had taught her to "take it to the Lord." The expression always struck her funny, but not the act. She frequently prayed in the woods. It was the perfect kind of location to focus your thoughts.

"Please, God," she murmured, "bring him back. Let him be like he used to be even if it's without Mom." A lump hardened in her throat and she fought back another urge to cry. But a moment later she opened her eyes and peered out into the rich greens and browns of the forest.

·2·

A Dangerous Crossing of Paths

Slats of sunlight drifted through the leaves like etched falls of water. Each ray appeared choked with the dust of the forest. Yet as Crista sniffed the warm air she noticed only the strong, leafy scent of sappy pine, boughy ash, and papery birch. She loved the odors of the woods. It reminded her of years past, when her mother was alive and the family took all those marvelous treks into the forest to ferret out wild blueberries and raspberries. Mom and Dad would belt out hymns or old "rock tunes," as they called them, and Crista soon learned to sing along.

Stretching, she thought that would be another drawing she would do one day, maybe after she had walked some.

She nestled a toe in a pile of brown leaves in a depression on the rock and flicked the leaves in the air, then caught one as it floated down in front of her eyes. "Why is he so far away all the time?" she murmured, thinking again about the sunken boat and her father's anger.

Her mother had understood. She had even painted pictures like Crista did now. And back then her father was so different. Crista's mother's voice came back into her mind: "She's going to be an artist, Jason. Better than I ever was."

Even then her father looked at the paintings and scribbles Crista did and hung them in his office. For a long time after the accident they hung there. Then one day he cleaned them all out. He said she was growing up and he wanted her more professional pieces. But finding them in the trash had hurt. She had cried then, but had said nothing to him about it.

She stood and jiggled her legs, shaking out the twitches. Then she picked up a leaf and crumpled it between her fingers. As the leaf cracked under the pressure, she thought about how she might bring the feeling of the forest into her art. That was the thing that fascinated her: putting onto a piece of paper with paint or ink or charcoal an image that made her feel what she had felt when she first saw it. That was the challenge. Miss Allison, her 5th grade teacher at Wallenpaupack Elementary, where she was in the sixth grade, encouraged her that she had struck on something that might make her a great artist someday. She would be in 6th grade that fall.

She didn't always show her work to her father. At least not now. He didn't ask about it, and, like the episode with the sunken pram, he sometimes blamed her interest in drawing for the trouble she got into.

Her father was a good doctor. He had been an obstetrician before Mother's accident, but afterward he turned to general practice. He had been doing it for almost the whole year now since her mother's death. He never told Crista why. More than once friends came by to talk to him about how they needed a baby doctor in the area. But her father would shrug and say, "I just can't do it now."

She had tried to piece it all together many times on these treks into the woods.

Crista brushed off the rock and sat down again, then gripped her knees and rocked back and forth on the huge elbow-shaped boulder.

From her perch she could see the large man-made lake in northeastern Pennsylvania where she lived: Lake Wallenpaupack. It was an Indian name, from the language of the Paupack Indians who once roamed and hunted in these woods. Many times Crista imagined herself an Indian princess riding a coal-black stallion and leading her people to victory over their enemies to the north and south.

Today, though, was not a day for little-girl dreams. "I just need to think for awhile," she said as she finally stood, running her fingers through her long, dark-brown hair. It came to the middle of her back, like her mother had wanted her to wear it. At times Crista thought she was pretty like her mother had been. But no one had said that to her lately, now that she wanted them to. She thought her dark eyebrows and long eyelashes were her best feature.

But her golden eyes were what her mother said made her look like a princess. Her eyes were not yellow, but an ochre color—gold, really. She had never seen anyone, not even Mother, with eyes like hers. At times she had caught people gazing at her with a kind of awe written all over their faces. Now she wondered if she really was pretty, if any boy would ever notice her.

She swung the backpack up and pulled the straps over her sunburned shoulders. "It doesn't matter," she murmured out loud. "'Beauty's only skin deep,'" her mother used to say. "What matters is who you are, what you are inside."

Her mother always emphasized character—"the precious quality of a quiet and gentle spirit"—a passage she often quoted which Crista knew was somewhere in the Bible. Her father rarely mentioned those things anymore.

She jumped down from the rock and wiped the tears away with her sleeve. Her buckskin moccasins gave her feet the feel of the earth. She liked that. They were a gift from an uncle who had shot a deer and had the hide tanned. She loved to squish her toes down into the loam of the forest soil. Stealing down a path silently in those moccasins made her feel more like an Indian princess than ever.

She began climbing the trail up the mountain. The sunlight warmed the air in the forest, but it was not so hot that you couldn't breathe. It was still the end of summer—plenty of time before the heavy snows would make the forest off limits except in snowshoes.

As she walked, she spotted some mountain laurel growing by the path. She took out her penknife and cut a few branches of the thick, rubbery leaves and quickly wove them into a circle. She put the crown on her head and made a brief bow.

"My lord," she said in a sweet voice, thinking of addressing a bearded King Arthur, or perhaps some Indian prince.

She answered in a gruff, manly voice. "Milady, have you come from the forest?"

"Yes, bearing sweets, my lord."

Crista closed her eyes and imagined the muscular arms of some dashing knight in armor sweeping her to his lips. She laughed.

When she was done, she rolled her eyes. "Mama would really think I've lost it," she said out loud, and continued up the path.

She always carried a penknife in the woods, and sometimes her father's hunting knife, though she didn't have it now. Usually she also brought something to eat and a flashlight in case the sun went down before she reached the main road to home. People said there were black bear in the woods. She thought she had seen one at a distance once, though she couldn't be sure. It might have been the light. Of course, there were plenty of fox and deer.

The real trouble, though, were the dump dogs. On the other side of the mountain, much to her disgust, lay the town dump. Once a week the people on the lake brought their trash to the dump. A fire always burned. Rats hid in its nooks and pockets. And mongrelly dump dogs—wild, crazy-looking beasts that had no manners and could be dangerous—roamed about scrounging for food. Several of the residents on the lake threatened to take up their guns and hunt them down to the last one. But no one had ever had the gumption to actually do it.

Crista was glad. Dump dogs or not, they were still dogs. She was sure they could be tamed if treated properly. They had all belonged to somebody at one time.

She wound along the trail, singing and picking at hanging boughs. She noticed some blue and red flowers growing by the trail and stooped to touch them. She didn't always pick flowers, knowing it would kill them. But she thought one or two might adorn her laurel crown, so she took it off and wove them onto the leafy circlet.

A gentle wind rustled the tops of the trees about her, and she stood, pleasantly startled. It would be a half-hour before she reached the top of the mountain. For the last few weeks she had tried to think of a name for the pineneedle-covered peak, even though it was more like an outsize hump. But she never hit on a name she liked.

She shuffled happily up the path. As usual, the woods freed her from the cares of home, family, and nearly everything else. The trail curved to the right ahead of her. She thought of the cupcakes again and stopped, pulling the crinkly package out of her backpack. Licking her lips, she opened the three creamy chocolate cupcakes and peeled one off, making sure none of the icing stuck to the cellophane. Then she turned the cake icing-down and took a bite. The chocolate sent shivers of sweet, tingly flavor through her mouth and into the pit of her stomach.

"Nothing like a cupcake on a walk through the forest," she said with a giggle. She unscrewed the cap of her canteen and drank down a cool slug of grape juice. It was a beautiful feeling. Here in the forest she felt free, alive, herself.

She had just recapped the canteen when behind her there was a sudden crack. The forest was always full of strange noises, and Crista turned without fear, still clutching the cakes. Onto the path stepped a huge white dog, a Great Dane—less than 40 feet away.

Crista froze. One of the dump dogs. *Don't move*, she told herself. *Maybe he doesn't see you. Maybe there's someone with him.* Her heart seemed to be banging through her rib cage.

The dog turned in her direction, fixing on her with an interested gaze.

It'll be all right, he's friendly, Crista thought again. She remained silent, rooted in place.

As the Dane's blue eyes blinked and skimmed up and down her figure, he flicked out his tongue with a wet slurp and growled. Crista glanced left and right to see if anyone else was with him. But she heard no one. "Nice dog," she said.

The dog bared its teeth, growling now deep in its throat. Somewhere Crista had read that this was a dog's way of warning enemies away without threatening attack. But she couldn't be sure.

She backed up. The Dane stepped toward her, sniffing, then stopping and giving a thick throated bark into the air. She quickly calculated that just standing normally his head reached as high as her throat. For a moment she could picture those huge white teeth tearing into her neck.

"Nice dog," she said again, swallowing, trying to think of which way to go. With the dog blocking the way back, the path only went up. She was no match for the quick strides of a Great Dane.

She inched backward, saying, "Nice dog. You're just alone, that's all. I know you're a nice dog."

The dog trotted forward a few paces, then planted both front feet and barked, throwing his head back regally and powerfully.

"What can I do?" Crista murmured, trying to calm the storm in her mind. Immediately she thought of the cupcakes in her hand. That might help. As she stepped back, she held out the chunks of brown cake, then pitched one to the ground a few feet in front of the dog. Without hesitation it leaped forward and scarfed the cupcake in a second, throwing his head back again and chewing it with gusto. If she wasn't so afraid, she would have laughed at how he slobbered all over it with such relish.

When he was finished, he gazed at her again, not moving. His eyes were a crystal blue. Beautiful. He was closer, but he wasn't growling, just watching her with those eager, almost electric eyes.

Crista stooped, gently laid the last chocolate cupcake on the ground in front of her, and then stepped calmly off into the woods. The dog advanced slowly, keeping to the right while she tiptoed off to the left of the trail. As he drew closer to the cupcake, she strode faster around until she was behind him. He lapped up the cupcake and thumped down on thin haunches, panting. For the first time Crista noticed his ribs showing under the dirty white coat. He was probably hungry.

To eat me, she thought again, her heart still pounding.

She hurried through the woods and joined the trail a hundred feet below the Dane. Looking back, she saw that the dog didn't follow. Then as she turned the corner, the dog fell out of sight. She walked stiff-legged, telling herself not to run. Not yet.

Then the dog barked. Loud. A sharp, menacing woof. Or was it a thank-you?

Crista didn't wait to find out. She hit sprint in less than a second. Her moccasins slapped the dirt on the trail. As she ran, she listened with terror for the sound of pursuit. But there was nothing. When she reached the highway across from her house, she stopped and turned around, her heart still hammering, her lungs burning.

The dog was gone.

"Thank you," she whispered with a closed-eye sigh, then sped across the highway. She didn't stop till she reached the front door of the cabin and had closed it behind her.

·3·

The Hidden Cabin

Crista didn't tell her father about the dog. He didn't seem upset about the boat any longer and she caught him looking silently off into space several times. That night she had a nightmare in which the Great Dane turned into a huge rock, and then the rock transposed into a monster with razor claws and huge fangs. She woke up in a sweat.

The next day her father didn't notice her unusual silence. Normally she chattered about something just to fill the nervous quiet. But he simply perused his medical magazines and that afternoon fell asleep in his green lounger, his Franklin glasses ready to topple off the end of his nose.

She prepared dinner the second night—hamburgers and fresh corn—with her usual perfection. However, when she was alone, she caught herself shaking several times. She repeatedly wondered if the dog would have attacked had she not given him the cupcake.

The fear passed, though, and after two days she told herself there really was nothing to be afraid of. The Great Dane probably had nightmares about *her*! She laughed about it, realizing that the dog might even be friendly if she was kind to him. He had such beautiful eyes, too. She spent an hour drawing his face and eyes, trying to find the right combination of blues to get that electric sheen.

Nonetheless, when she went back to the woods, she took precautions. That Saturday she carried not only her penknife but also her father's hunting knife on her belt for easy and ready access. He had let her use the big knife for the last two years when she went on her long walks. But she said nothing because if he knew about the dog, he might have forbidden her from even going into the woods at all. He rarely arrived home before 6:30, even on Saturdays, when he made hospital calls all day. And she knew she would be making dinner well before that, safe in their kitchen.

It was a two- or three-mile hike all the way around the mountain, and she rarely took that route. Usually she trekked to the top, had lunch, then wound her way off the trail back down. It was fun finding new routes and ways through the huge rocks that covered the landscape.

Scuffling up the trail, she kept a sharp eye peeled for any signs of dump dogs. She almost wished one would show—just to be able to brandish the shiny, bone-handled knife. But only the tweets of birds and the buzzes of a few insects stirred the quiet of the woods.

She carried two packs of cupakes in her pack this time. If she did meet the Dane, she would have one for him too, and wouldn't have to sacrifice all her pleasure for another daring escape! She had also wrapped up a bologna sandwich with lettuce and tomato, a Slim Jim, a bag of skinned carrots, and a canteen full of strawberry Kool-Aid. She planned to follow the mountain trail all the way across its face, something she hadn't done yet that summer. She knew a deserted hunter's cabin sat in the nook between the mountains. She could have lunch there and possibly get some ideas for a new drawing.

Crista rubbed the sweat off her forehead. She felt hot and sticky and took several swigs from her canteen as she hiked along.

Then as she plodded around the bend in the trail near the descent to the cabin, she was surprised to see a stream of smoke wafting skyward. "Somebody's there!" she said out loud. Her voice startled her, and she glanced around the woods thinking some ghostly creature might jump out at her. But all was quiet.

"Who on earth could be there?" she murmured. "It's not even hunting season."

She decided to be cautious. No reason to let them know I'm here, she reasoned. There was no telling who they were. And her father had frequently warned her of consorting with strangers, or placing herself in unnecessary danger.

Her moccasins swished on the trail. She wended her way carefully now, dancing around twigs and scurrying by with effortless silence. The old blood-banging feeling of adventure gripped her as she moved silently from tree to tree imagining herself a daring Indian princess. She wanted to see, but she didn't want to be seen.

The woods thinned out slightly. A moment later she spotted the cabin in the clearing. Sure enough, a wisp of whitish smoke streamed from the cobblestone chimney. A shiny red pickup truck sat parked in the yard at the far end.

Crista knelt down and surveyed the whole scene. No one appeared in the yard. She instinctively picked up a twig and rolled it between her thumb and finger. What to do now? She imagined she was Nancy Drew spying out the enemy. But deep down she hoped whoever lived there wouldn't be an enemy.

The cabin stood on the edge of a small brook. Crista heard the water gurgling over the stony bottom, only inches deep. She breathed quietly and did not feel afraid, just expectant.

The cabin front was built of logs probably fashioned from trees felled to make the clearing. But the back of the little house was gray barnwood, perhaps hauled up from some nearby farm. Crista had seen the place before, but never occupied.

She wondered if she should get closer. Then the front door opened with a rusty squeak.

Crista immediately ducked down and sprawled on the dirt, then shaded her eyes with her hand. A woman in a gingham dress stepped out into the sunlight. She had long blonde hair. Her face was sunburned. Even at a distance, Crista could tell she was pretty. And not that much older than she was.

The woman dragged out a basket, then hefted it to her waist and carried it behind the cabin. Quickly following her line of progress, Crista noticed a clothesline hanging raggedly between two trees in the yard.

Who could she be? Crista wondered. She decided she had to get closer.

In a crouch, she scrambled down the trail in the cover of the leafy trees. Her pack bounced on her back and she reached behind her as she ran, holding it tight against her body. She came out below the woman, near the creek. The girl sang to herself and hung the clothing—towels, two pairs of blue jeans, and some shirts—over the clothesline.

Crista didn't recognize the song, and the girl didn't appear dangerous, but Crista wasn't sure what to do. Once her youth group at church had taken a trip to New Jersey, where the leader had told a story about people called "Pineys," people who lived in the lonely wooded pine forests of New Jersey. He told hair-raising stories about how they could sneak up on you and chop your head in half with a hatchet. Or how they might cut your throat if you weren't looking. But Crista had never heard of such a thing by the lake.

The girl started a new song, this time something Crista recognized, a song called "Boys of Summer." Crista had heard it before on the radio. The girl stuck several clothespins in her mouth. Crista liked the way her lips curved. Her blonde hair reminded Crista of some of the beautiful girls she had seen at the beach once when her mom and dad took her to Ocean City, New Jersey, on a vacation.

She knew she had to do something. It wasn't fair to hide like this, watching her like some Peeping Tom. She wouldn't want someone peeping in on her. Finally, swallowing away her fear, she stood and waited, tugging at her long brown hair, hoping it didn't look too bad. When the girl didn't notice her, she called "Hello" and waved hesitantly.

The girl jumped the moment she heard the voice, but after she found Crista standing between the trees she smiled. "Hi, there! You scared me."

"I didn't mean to." Crista smiled and shifted on her feet, wondering if the girl would invite her over.

Stepping out from behind the clothing on the line, the girl wiped herself with her apron and said cheerfully, "We don't have many visitors here."

Crista shuffled forward a few paces. "Mind if I come on over?"

The girl glanced around. "Sure, I guess Johnny won't mind."

Brushing aside a branch, Crista strolled out into the open. The woman was barefoot and the dress was torn. Pretty poor, Crista thought, and wondered if she might bring them some of the strawberry jam she had made in the late spring when the berries were full and ripe.

"My name's Crista Mayfield. I live over by the lake."

"Nadine Semms," the girl said. "You look about 13."

"Twelve," Crista said shyly. "But thanks anyway."

Nadine smiled broadly. She had a wide, pretty mouth that lit up her whole face when she smiled. "Would you like a drink? We don't have much, but it's cool and fresh."

Crista looked Nadine up and down. She had to be less than 20, she thought. She might still be in high school. Nadine's eyes were a radiant green. In the light, her white-blonde hair almost sparkled. But the drab dress made her look like someone from *Little House on the Prairie*.

"Do you live here?" Crista asked. "I thought this was a hunting cabin."

Nadine pursed her lips suddenly and put her finger up to it mischievously. "It is. Johnny's uncle used to own it and sold it to Johnny for nearly nothing. It hasn't been used in years. It took me two weeks just to clean it up. Come on in, I'll show you."

Crista followed her. Already she liked Nadine, whoever she was. She seemed friendly enough. Was Johnny her husband? She didn't know. But she was curious to find out, and possibly make some new friends.

·4·

Great Hopes

Nadine led Crista toward the rustic cabin. The worn green shingles on the roof looked like they might flap wings and fly off any minute. Bark-stripped whitish logs nailed in rows covered the front, while the sides and back were gray knotty barnwood. Someone had punched out a few of the knotholes and stuffed them with mud or perhaps some kind of plaster.

As they stepped onto the porch, Crista stared at the moth-eaten deerhead hanging over the door. Nadine remarked, "I've been trying to get Johnny to take that thing down ever since we got here, but he won't." She giggled, a happy, wide-eyed kind of giggle that Crista liked.

"How long have you been here now?" Crista asked, as they both stepped through the heavy wide door made of thick slabs of oak.

"Since last month," Nadine said. She pulled a chair out from under a rickety table. The main room was pretty and well lit with a small fire burning in the fireplace. Nadine had brought a woman's touch to the place. One long log spanned the room over their heads in the middle. It was a typical pattern of cabins in the area. One big log like that held the whole house together. The log was shiny—lacquered, Crista knew, from her art experience—full of knots, and handsome. Crista loved the look immediately.

To the far right was a kitchen, with no refrigerator, but just a big ice chest, two white metal cabinets, a sink, and some cupboards. Blue dishes lay drying on the side of the sink.

"Do you have running water?" Crista asked. She didn't think it could be possible.

"Yeah, I run down to the brook and back." Nadine chuckled again.

Crista smiled at her joke.

Nadine sighed wistfully. "I'm glad someone can laugh about it. If I couldn't laugh, I'd probably cry."

She gazed at Crista with a big smile, then looked away. "After that, I sterilize it in the fireplace." She pointed to the greystone fireplace against the wall. "That's why we have a fire going."

A rickety stairway led up to a cozy-looking loft. Crista supposed the room in the back was the bedroom. There were some old chairs, a couch, and a small card table in the "living room," but it was really one main room with the bedroom in the back and the loft. Three more deerheads hung over the fireplace, with some squirrels, rabbits, and a fox on the sides. A large fish also stared out from another plaque over a window. Its mouth was open with a row of tiny white teeth. Crista knew it was too big for a bass, and it wasn't a pickerel or a pike. Maybe a walleyed pike, she thought. She had seen them in the fish books that her father kept in their little library at home. She had even drawn a few.

"It's a nice little cabin," Crista said after giving it the once-over. "Real nice."

"It's home," Nadine commented, cocking her head and nodding. "All we've got, I guess."

Crista wasn't sure how to approach the subject, but finally she said, "What are you doing here?"

Raising her blonde eyebrows mysteriously, Nadine answered, "Just starting out in life. Everybody has to start somewhere. We're here." She grinned and looked around. "I know it's not much . . ."

"Oh, it's great," Crista interrupted. "I can tell you really love it. So that's what counts."

Nodding, Nadine's lips crinkled into a wry smile. "Not what I'm used to, I suppose, but what can I say? Anyway, tell me about you. And sit down, please. Would you like something to drink? Johnny brought back some colas from the stream. The stream keeps things fairly cold."

Crista didn't want to contribute to making Nadine poorer than she already was, but she also didn't want to be rude. Finally she said, "I'd love one."

Popping off the cap, Nadine set a six-ounce Coke bottle in front of Crista, then opened another one for herself. She plunked down into the seat and gazed at Crista. "So what are you all about, Crista Mayfield?"

There wasn't much to tell. Crista told Nadine about her father and how she often took walks in the woods, what it was like going to school in the lake area, and how she had run into the dog.

"Those dogs," Nadine snorted. "They're always snuffling around. I've seen that big one. He can be mean, too. You'd better watch out."

Crista patted her hunting knife. "That's why I take this."

"Good idea." Nadine slit her eyes. "But by the time you get it out, he could have your throat."

The air of the cabin was warm, but comfortable. Crista noticed a fishy smell and thought Nadine must have cooked some lake catfish, bass, or sunnies for lunch. Crista said, "I don't think the big one's mean, actually. In fact, I even kind of hoped I'd run into him again."

"What on earth for?" Nadine's green eyes sparkled in the light coming in through the door and the windows. Her wavy blonde hair hung like a beautiful waterfall down her back. Crista almost wished Nadine would let her comb it.

"Oh, tame him, maybe," Crista said. "I'd like to have a pet—if Daddy would let me."

"Sounds like your dad doesn't let you do much."

"Oh, he lets me do pretty much what I want—the stuff he doesn't know about, anyway." She smiled and rolled her eyes. "He's very quiet. I think deep down inside he still..." Crista winced, "hurts, I guess."

"How come?" Nadine sipped her Coke, then cupped her chin in her hands with her elbows on the table. Crista thought she had such sincere eyes. She sensed that Nadine liked her. It was a good feeling.

"I don't know. Well, yeah, I do." Her throat caught a moment, then the feeling vanished. "My mother."

Nadine paused, gazing intently at Crista. "I take it your mother's not around."

"She died just about a year ago."

"I'm sorry." The girl instinctively reached across and pressed Crista's hand. It was a friendly, caring gesture, and Crista liked it.

"It was my fault," Crista said suddenly, startled at the tears that came to her eyes and the huskiness that came back into her voice.

Looking at her sympathetically, Nadine's brow creased. She waited as Crista regained her composure. Then Nadine shook her head. "You're just a kid, Crista. How could it have been your fault?"

Crista sighed. She wasn't sure Nadine would really want to hear the story. But something about Nadine's wide-eyed friendliness made her want to. "I was playing around, razzing my mom while we were shopping. I stepped into the street. There was a line of empty parking spaces, but it was still the street. Then a car came down fast, out of control. Mom turned and screamed. My back was to the car. I was standing there looking at her, wondering what the problem was. She leaped to knock me out of the way . . ."

Clearing her throat, Crista fought back the rising guilt and grief. She bit her lip and Nadine said, "It's all right, you don't have to talk about it."

Shaking her head, Crista said, "No, it helps. My mom knocked me out of the way. The car came all the way up on the curb and crashed into a store. But she was hit. Head-on."

Nadine winced, then squeezed Crista's hand. "I bet it hurts a lot."

Crista nodded, suddenly unable to speak. She looked away, forcing her eyes to focus on something else. "If my dad would just say something about it. If he'd just say, 'It's your fault, Crista!' I could live with it. But I don't know what he thinks or anything."

Nadine's eyes glimmered with tears and she gripped Crista's hand. "Men are like that, Crista. You shouldn't let your mind run wild with all the possibilities."

"But what am I supposed to do?" Crista suddenly said with a sigh. Then she shook her head. "I just have to live with it—that's all." She gazed at the bright blue-and-yellow curtains around the windows. "You've decorated the house nicely." She wanted to change the subject.

"Considering what I had to work with," Nadine answered with a shrug. Crista could tell she was proud of her efforts, though.

They both sipped their Cokes for a few seconds, looking around the room, Crista with curiosity and Nadine with obvious pride and happiness. Then she said, "Crista, anytime you want to talk about it, you can talk to me. Okay?"

Crista nodded. "Thanks." She already felt like she and Nadine were friends.

Then Nadine said, "Can I tell you a secret?"

Crista leveled her eyes on Nadine. Her heart almost stopped as she realized Nadine also wanted to tell her something personal and deep. She said, "Are you sure you want to?"

Nadine nodded. "I have to tell somebody besides Johnny."

"Okay."

"I'm pregnant."

A tiny crackle of thrill shot through Crista as she gazed into Nadine's radiant face. All her life she had heard from her mother how precious and how beautiful it had been to have her as her own baby. It was something, even with her mom gone, that she sometimes dreamed about herself. Crista couldn't help letting a huge grin explode onto her face. "That's so great!"

Nadine nodded her head quickly with wide eyes. "I figure I'm due in January. Maybe January 1. Can't you see I'm showing?" She looked down at her belly.

Crista's eyes followed hers. They both burst out laughing. Nadine's billowy dress wouldn't have let her show if she was Two Ton Tessie. Nadine said, "Guess I need to visit Macy's or someplace, huh?"

They both laughed again.

"Anyway," Nadine said, "I am. And I know I'm showing, even if no one else says so, especially Johnny. He says I'm the most beautiful girl on earth and even if I was showing it wouldn't bother him. Isn't that great?"

The excitement rushed through Crista and she suddenly wondered if Nadine might let her babysit and things like that. It would be wonderful to have a friend who had a real baby. The joy jumped and banged around inside her as she and Nadine continued talking. Here it was, just the beginning of school, and already a great thing had happened to her. She thought maybe things weren't as bad as it had looked earlier.

"So what will you name him . . . or her," Crista asked excitedly.

"If it's a boy, John Junior—that's settled," Nadine replied. "I like that. I think it's right. That's kind of a family tradition in Johnny's family. But if it's a girl . . ." Her voice took on a mysterious whisper. "I want to name her Fairlight."

Crista was almost too shocked to answer. She had never heard such a name.

Shrugging slightly, Nadine said, "I know . . . it sounds strange. But it's a name from a favorite book of mine called *Christy* and I've always liked it. It wouldn't be her regular name, just what I'd call her when I'm being especially tender. You know what I mean? Her given name will be Rebekah. Rebekah Fairlight."

"I like it," Crista said immediately, rolling the name over in her mind. "I really like it."

"Do you?"

"Yes!"

They both laughed and Nadine shook her head with wonder, a wide smile etching her face. "You do, I can tell. You really do like it."

As they laughed, there was a sound outside, some-one whistling. Nadine jumped up. "It's Johnny," she said. "I hope he caught something." Boots crunched on the gravel driveway.

Crista was about to get up, but Nadine said, "Sit. Let him walk in and be surprised. He's as hard up for a friend as I am."

Waiting, her hands in her lap, Crista watched the doorway. The boots clattered on the stone steps and then he was standing between the doorposts in the light. He was tall and lanky, with a bit of a beard and a Phillies baseball cap on. Thick, black hair poked out from under the red cap. He looked like a basketball player. He took one look around at everyone and said, "Well, messengers from the end of the earth, no doubt." He swung out a clipline with the horde of fish on it—sunnies, bass, cat. "I caught a dinner, Babe."

Nadine jumped up and hugged him. "Johnny, this is Crista Mayfield. She's 12 and she lives on the lake. Crista, say hello to Johnny Semms, my wonderful hus-band."

Gulping at Johnny's boyish good looks, Crista stood, suddenly feeling very small. Johnny draped out his huge hand. Crista took it, and Johnny squeezed her hand lightly and said, "Welcome to our little shack." He smelled of fish and his fingers were damp.

Instantly Crista liked his voice. It was manly, but he was obviously about the same age as Nadine. Crista still wasn't sure what that was, but it couldn't have been more than 20.

Nadine took the string of fish. "This'll be a great dinner for tonight. Are you going to clean them, Honey?"

"Sure," Johnny said.

Brushing off her dress and dropping the fish into the sink, Nadine suddenly turned around and looked at Crista. "You could stay for dinner if you want."

Crista shook her head. "I really think I'd better be going. I told my dad I'd make dinner tonight. It's my turn. He and I switch nights, and he wouldn't like it too much if I didn't show up."

Nadine smiled and poked Johnny in the side. The big man wriggled away and Nadine said, "I understand. I wouldn't like it if Johnny didn't show up with his load of fish either."

The air seemed to buzz between Johnny and Nadine, and Crista could tell they were deeply in love. Johnny stepped out of the doorway. "Don't rush off because of me. I'll be glad to drive you down the road."

"No, I'd really better be going," Crista said. "But it was fun meeting you. It was nice to get to know someone new."

Nadine said, "You'll come again?" Her eyes had a hopeful look that made Crista feel warm.

She nodded. "If you want, I can come by tomorrow."

"I'd love it." Nadine looked at Johnny and he nodded in approval.

Crista stepped through the doorway, feeling like she was interrupting the last of the romantic lovers in a special moment. Nadine said, "Watch out for the those dogs."

"Don't worry about me," Crista said with a wave. She walked back toward the woods. When she reached the edge, she turned and said, "Thanks for the Coke."

Nadine and Johnny stood on the porch. He had his arm around her shoulders, gripping her close. She waved. "Anytime."

Heading off down the road, Crista felt happy she had made a new friend. "Going to have a baby," she whispered, and that crackly joy shot through her again. "I could babysit and make a little dress and maybe Daddy would even deliver..."

She cut herself off. No, her father had already said he would never deliver babies again. She swallowed and sighed. "Well, even if it isn't him who brings the baby into the world, it'll be just as glorious," she said with finality.

"I could even draw a picture of them," Crista said again as she jogged down the trail now, so full of excitement she thought she would scream.

·5·

Almost Too Late

As Crista hurried off through the woods, her heart overflowed with a rushing feeling of happiness, like the sound of water in a stream as the snow melted. She whispered, "That was so fun, Lord. Will Nadine and Johnny and me really be friends?"

She added, "Please make that happen, Lord. Please."

As she turned a corner, she felt that it *would* happen, that God would make sure of it. She bunched her fist and shook it at her sides in a gesture of security.

Crista had become a Christian less than six months earlier during a series of special evangelistic services in church. She had prayed, and from that time Jesus became a real and close friend, though He didn't always seem so near. Somehow, though, she always knew He was there with her wherever she was. She didn't think a lot about it. The inner feeling was just there and she couldn't easily explain it.

Her father agreed when she asked to be baptized, but he hadn't shown much excitement about it, and she was surprised that he didn't. Her mother often read her Bible stories and the family always went to

church together, though her father had become
rather irregular in the last year.

Yet Crista was sure her dad was a Christian. They
always said grace at meals. Sometimes she caught him
praying on his knees in his bedroom. She would tiptoe
away, hoping he hadn't seen her. But it gave her a good
feeling to see him praying like that. He had frequently
prayed with her each night before bed, before her
mother was killed. But after the funeral he became
less regular, even though he always asked her to make
sure *she* prayed before she went to sleep.

As she blinked in the afternoon sunlight, Crista's
moccasins felt cool on the mossy trail. Several times
she stopped and listened, but the woods were quiet.
She shuffled along, musing and singing to herself.

Then she saw it, 40 yards down the trail—a doe and
a fawn just beginning to lose its spots. The doe had
obviously caught Crista's scent. She stood postcard
still, the doe's great dark brown eyes fixed on Crista's
face. Crista didn't move. They looked like they had
been running and had stopped when they saw her.

She watched as the fawn nuzzled her mother. It was
a beautiful sight. Picture beautiful.

Then to her right she suddenly heard barking. The
doe's frightened eyes flickered and she leaped into the
woods with the fawn right behind her. They both
bounced forward, obviously terrified.

Moments later four dump dogs scrambled up the
trail, barking and yelping, hot on the scent of the deer.

Crista's heart thundered into her throat and she
cried, "God, don't let them get the fawn, please!"

Two gray-haired mongrels dashed through the
woods. They weren't big, only up to Crista's thigh, but

big enough with four of them to bring down a deer. Following them was a black-haired Lab and a brown spaniel of some sort with white spots. They all appeared vicious, their lips wet with foam. Their human families, if they ever had them, were only a memory of years gone by. They were as wild as the deer.

Crista watched in terror as the four dogs spread out and homed in on the two helpless deer. The dogs obviously knew how to hunt. The two grays galloped around to the left behind the deer, cutting off the only route of escape straight ahead, up the mountain. There it was rocky and hard going, even for a deer.

Instinctively Crista pulled out her hunting knife. "They're not getting that fawn." She gritted her teeth and sprinted up the path, following the trail. The dogs howled behind the fawn. Crista could see that the little one had fallen behind.

A branch lashed her face as Crista veered off into the woods, leaving the matted trail. She told herself the dogs wouldn't turn on her, praying that it was true. But she couldn't let them get to the fawn.

Two gray streaks shot way ahead of her, bounding through the woods with full-throated howls. The black-haired dog circled above the deer. Crista knew he would drive them back, right into the jaws of the other three.

The doe suddenly stopped, jerking its head around looking for the fawn and sniffing the air. Was there a buck somewhere nearby? That's what they needed—a buck with a big rack, Crista thought. He'd put those dogs in their places.

But no buck appeared.

The fawn made a mewling noise. Immediately the doe turned, bounded back, and butted her head on the fawn's rump. The fawn mewled again, in a way that reminded Crista of a kitten. It had stopped dead still. Moments later the dogs surrounded the doe and fawn, closing in.

Crista crashed through the woods, shouting, "No! Stop, you mongrels!" She waved the knife threateningly in front of her. Her feet bruised in the thin moccasins as they slammed down on roots and rocks.

"Stop it!"

The dogs barked, baring their teeth, and rushed in upon the doe, nipping at her flanks. The fawn cowered next to its mother, shivering. They both stood in a small clearing. Large scattered rocks, rotting stumps, and a thick blanket of pine needles enclosed the area. The fawn's foot seemed to be caught.

Crista rushed blindly through the woods, screaming louder, "No! Get away!" But the dogs only darted back and forth, snapping at the doe as she kicked, trying to catch one of the dogs in the teeth. The mother put her head down, butting in different directions, but she had no antlers. The dogs weren't afraid at all.

Then the big black mongrel that looked part Lab and part German shepherd bolted at the fawn. The big dog struck the fawn's leg and bowled it over. The fawn opened its mouth in fear, but nothing came out. The doe wheeled, kicking the dog in the side, rolling him over. Immediately all three of the others raged in upon them, sensing a kill. The doe churned her legs in panic.

Crista reached the rocks. "Go away!" she yelled again, brandishing the knife. She thought about throwing it, but that would just waste it. What else was there to do? The black rushed at the doe, biting it hard in the leg. A patch of red appeared in the brown fur as the doe kicked the dog away.

"No!" Crista screamed and leaped at the nearest dog, battering him with her foot in the gut. It rolled over, bared its teeth, and rushed at her, stopping only two feet from the tip of her knife, growling.

Then the other gray dog turned and snapped at her. Still, they did not attack. Crista thought they might have seen knives before. The gray mongrel, after gazing at her fiercely, turned back to the fawn.

Crista yelled again, but they paid no attention. One of the dogs had the doe's leg now and shook his head viciously. Another bit at the fawn. The young one pawed at the ground, trying to push itself up. Its huge brown eyes darted wildly with fright.

Spotting a rock, Crista grabbed it and threw it at the lead dog, the black. It bounced off his right haunch.

The black whipped around and growled, then advanced slowly on Crista. She backed up, holding the knife out in front of her. "You come at me and I'll stab you. Get away. Get away from that fawn."

The doe tried to kick at the other three dogs while the black mongrel advanced on Crista. The dog pulled its black gums back, showing three long fangs. One was missing.

Crista fought back a feeling of dizziness and terror. She backed up, waving the knife in the dog's face. "I'll cut your eyes out, you beast. I'll cut them out and boil them."

The dog only edged closer. She knew it would rush her if she didn't do something. Then her left heel hit a stump and caught in the vee of two roots. She jerked at it and her moccasin flipped off. She fell backward.

She knew the dog would be on her, but suddenly she caught a branch with her left hand. It didn't break. She got her balance just in time.

The dog leaped forward and she jabbed the sharp knife at him. He stopped just before being cut.

Crista saw that the doe was losing the battle. One of the gray mutts bit at the doe's haunch and the other two circled, trying to get at the fawn. She gave him a kick in the teeth and he yelped. But they weren't giving up. The doe's breathing came in sharp rasps.

Crista realized she couldn't keep backing up. She suddenly shouted, "Help! Somebody! Please help!"

The dog had her. It advanced with its head down, ready to bite her. She waved the knife at the black-haired mongrel and bent down to pick up a rock. "Go! Get out of here!" She threw the rock at the dog's head. It leaped nimbly out of the way. But it moved back.

Then she lunged at him again with the knife. The dog wheeled backward, almost tripping over himself.

"There. See. You're not so brave."

Crista took another step, jabbing toward it with the knife. "Go away. Now!" She picked up another rock.

The dog howled, as if making a signal.

Instantly the two other gray-haired mutts joined him, circling her. Crista's heart seemed to be right in her throat. There was no route of escape now. One of the grays got behind her. The black advanced menacingly. She waved the knife. The other brown-haired dog held onto the doe.

Then the two dogs in front of her threw back their ears and turned to look at something behind Crista. She heard a wild thrashing behind her. Out of the corner of her eye a huge patch of white blitzed into the rock strewn area, barking. It was the white Dane from the other day!

The Dane snapped at the gray mutt behind Crista, sending him yelping off through the woods. The black backed off with the other gray. The white Dane sank his huge jaw into the rear end of the brown spaniel on the doe. It rolled over and fought, trying to get at the Dane's throat. The black came in behind him and nipped at his calf. But the Dane had the spaniel by the neck. Crista knew a huge dog like that could tear out the smaller dog's throat. She could see the dog knew it too. It's eyes swiveled helplessly and it whimpered.

The Dane pinned the dog to the ground. It's really going to tear out its throat, Crista thought in horror.

But suddenly the spaniel froze, as if unable to breathe. It let out a bloodcurdling yelp.

The Dane let it go. The spaniel jumped up and limped off into the woods without looking back. It breathed with a rough hacking sound.

The doe and fawn still stood, unmoving, blood on both their flanks.

But the Dane had only started. As it turned, the black Lab bared its fangs. The Dane moved toward it. After a pause, the Lab turned and ran. The two grays followed, their whippy, hard tails between their legs.

In a moment just Crista, the Great Dane, and the doe and fawn stood alone, all panting with weariness.

The fawn's flank was covered with blood and froth. The doe's hind leg was also bleeding. But she sniffed the air, getting her bearings. She moved forward on wobbly legs, then nosed at the fawn.

The Dane panted and watched. It stood only a few feet away, but the doe did not seem to be afraid. Crista wiped at her forehead, still holding the knife, her heart still hammering. Her eyes burned with tears. "Thank you," she said. "Thank you."

The Dane stared at her with his huge blue eyes, then sniffed and looked around majestically.

The doe turned and staggered off with the fawn following. They went in the opposite direction from the other dogs. Crista and the Dane watched until they were out of sight. "Please find your mate," Crista whispered.

When she said it, the Dane laid its ears back on his head a moment, then he turned to eye her again.

Crista's heart hammered against her chestbone. "So it's you and me again," she said.

The Dane didn't move.

Crista hesitated a moment, then placed the knife back in its sheath. The other dogs had disappeared.

"I guess you're not such a bad guy after all," Crista said, suddenly smiling and wiping away her tears. "You're very handsome, you know."

The Dane sat back on its huge haunches, throwing its head back and letting the tongue loll out. Crista leaned back against the tree. The dog still didn't move, then nipped at a flank as if flicking off a bug. Its head came back around and stared at Crista a moment with those ice-blue eyes rimmed by red eyelids. It was a startling effect against the white hair. She suddenly realized that the dog was an albino.

Then Crista remembered. Immediately she pulled off her backpack, fumbling in it. She took out the pack of cupcakes, unwrapped them, and laid all three on the ground in front of her, then stepped back a few feet.

The Dane eyed her. The big red eyelids with the electric blue eyes were hard to get used to. Its pointy white ears moved back and forth like a radar antenna. Crista waited. She said, "It's okay. They're for you. To say thanks."

The Dane stood up, rolled out its tongue, threw back its head, and barked. A deep, throaty bellow.

Crista jerked with sudden fright.

But the big dog stepped forward, lapped up the first one, then the other two cupcakes. He threw his head back, casting the cupcake deep into his throat. He chomped them hungrily. Crista watched, wondering if she should try to pet him.

"You're very handsome," she said again.

The Dane woofed in a friendly way, then turned and trotted off in the direction of the fawn and doe, its large feet swishing along like a quiet, gallant warrior through his kingdom.

Crista didn't move. Twice the dog stopped, turned, and looked back at her. Crista thought maybe he was making sure the deer and fawn were all right. But she wasn't sure a dog could think that far ahead.

Then he disappeared into the woods.

As Crista stood still, hardly daring to breathe, the silence of the woods suddenly seemed eerie. Then just as suddenly the call of a bird broke the quiet and the wood instantly filled with a new chirping, the scurry of squirrels, and a jerky chipmunk making its way across a rock—as if everything had stopped until the matter had been settled.

Crista crumpled up the cellophane cover for the cupcakes and dropped it into her pack. She peered off through the green and brown tree-trunked wood. She could not see or hear any sign of the animals. She noticed for the first time that she was calm.

Then she walked to the stump and pulled her moccasin back on while sitting on a rock. "Rontu," she said. "I'm going to call you Rontu."

It was from a name in a book she had read about an Indian girl who survived alone on an island after all her people left. She had tamed a mongrel left on the island by seafarers and had named him Rontu. Crista had always liked the name—and the book.

"Now," she thought as she hurried down the trail, "I have my own Rontu."

But would he ever let her touch him?

"He's so handsome and beautiful and kingly," Crista murmured again, her eyes tearing. "I hope I'll see him again. I hope. I hope."

That night she excitedly told her father about seeing the deer and the dog without telling him about the fight. She didn't want to upset him, but she was worried more that he might forbid her from going into the woods at all. He listened with interested eyes, then said, "You have to be careful, Crissy. It can be dangerous."

"I will," she said as she looked into her lap. It was the first time in many months that he had listened to one of her stories all the way through. He turned back to the magazine he was reading. His brown hair had fallen over his forehead and the glasses were slightly slanted.

If only he would smile, Crista thought. That would be enough.

But he didn't.

Afterward he smoked his pipe in the chair and read the paper. Crista worked all evening on a drawing of

Nadine standing out at the clothesline. School would be starting on Tuesday, but she didn't really look forward to it, though at least her birthday was Wednesday. She wondered if her father would remember. He hadn't said a word about that either.

·6·

Red Blotches

On the Sunday and Monday before school opened, Crista visited Nadine and Johnny again. On each occasion she took some raw hamburger, hoping to offer it to Rontu. But she didn't see him. She left the meat at the corner of the trail where she had first met him, in front of a tree with two carved initials in it: "JF and BK." She called it "The Love Tree." She thought it might remind the dog of her.

On Tuesday school started. Crista entered sixth grade. Her teacher was Mr. Robbins, a short, thickset man with a heavy black mustache. He was new. He made a commanding entrance and rattled all the kids into complete obedience. Crista just hoped he would have at least a few artistic cells in his brain. But she knew they probably wouldn't start any art projects with Mrs. Bevans until next week, until all the fuss about arithmetic, spelling, English, and history had been squared away.

She began thinking about several collages and drawings she wanted to do. Each year the school PTA sponsored an art contest around Thanksgiving. She envisioned something made out of stones and slate from the beach for the collages, and some animal and people drawings.

On Wednesday morning at breakfast, her father pushed a little velvet case toward her plate as he sat down. "Happy birthday," he said.

Crista swallowed, astonished. He had remembered!

She flipped open the lid. It was a watch. The gold face with the numbers in Roman numerals was small with little jewels around the rim. She could tell it was an expensive watch. It was like her mother's—which her father had promised to give her when she turned 21.

She turned it over in her hand, thinking he might have had something engraved on it, like Mama's. But the back only said "Waterproof. Shockproof." It was a minor disappointment, but just that he remembered was enough.

When she looked up, he was gazing out the window.

"Thank you, Daddy."

He turned and nodded, a quick smile flickering then disappearing from his face.

She waited. "Can I give you a kiss?"

He nodded. "Of course."

She got up, hurried around the big oaken dining room table in front of the huge window that looked out over the lake, and gave him a quick peck. For a moment she wanted to hold on. His face smelled of shaving lotion and it was smooth except for his mustache. But they didn't normally kiss. His breath was scented with pipe smoke. Even a good toothbrushing never got rid of that.

She pulled back from him and sat down. She wore the traditional outfit for her school: blue jeans and a

T-shirt. After clasping the watch onto her wrist, she realized how small and foolish it looked with the rest of her outfit. This was a watch for dressing up, which they rarely did around the Mayfield home.

Still, he had remembered. That was more than enough.

As she started out the door, her father said, "I'll get a cake for dinner—with candles."

She turned in the doorway and smiled. "Oh, would you?"

"I already ordered it."

"Okay." Her heart was already drumming and she felt so happy she wanted to jump out of her skin. But she ran up the slate stone path to the road, then waved and hurried on, her throat suddenly tight. *Maybe he really does forgive me for the accident,* she told herself.

She caught the bus to school up at the corner of the dirt road that cut down into the trees along the houses along their part of the lake. She was greeted by catcalls and snickers from the boys. Sometimes she wished they would just grow up. But she took a seat beside a friend named Betsy Higgins. Betsy wore her long brown hair in braids, and her freckles had blended with her deep tan. They talked about the summer, then watched quietly as the bus rolled over the hills toward the sparkling elementary school on the other side of the lake. Crista decided to wear her watch to Nadine's place that afternoon.

At four o'clock, when the bus dropped her off at the end of the road to her home, Crista said goodbye to Betsy, promising to come over for a visit. Betsy lived several miles down the lake, so they didn't see each other that much.

Crista jogged down the dirt road, her jeans making raspy swishes as she ran. Once home, she filled her backback with two hot dogs wrapped in aluminum foil, a pair of binoculars, and some Ziplock bags for collecting stones and things for her collages. She strapped on the hunting knife after hesitating about it several times. Then she marched up the road to the trail across from the mailboxes at the highway.

When she entered the forest, her chest throbbed with excitement. School never gave her any real thrill like it did for some kids. She didn't get great grades, mostly because she didn't try. But in art she always excelled. Both her fourth-grade and fifth-grade teachers had entered her painting and other pieces in contests. Once she had taken a third in a local contest for kids in the whole lake region.

She pushed back a branch hanging over the trail. Ahead of her, several paper birches bent back from the trail. People liked to climb them. When they reached the top, the birch would bend down slowly, giving you a nice joyride. It was an airy, ferris-wheel kind of feeling. Crista stopped doing it when she learned that it killed the trees.

She stood on the trail and inhaled deeply, as if the air there was different—more powerful and energizing than that closer to home. It gave her a jolt of joy just to look down the dark trail, wondering what might happen today. In the woods, she felt at one with life. There she knew she was someone who mattered.

She looked both ways. As a car hurtled by on the main road, she began the climb toward the cleft to Nadine's cabin.

Twenty minutes later she stood at the edge of the clearing. She had not seen any animals on the way up.

But this time she left the hot dogs for Rontu at "The Love Tree," as she now called it, hoping maybe he would be there when she came back.

She shuffled quietly into the clearing, but no one was around. The red pickup truck was gone. She meandered around the stumps and stones lying about. *No clothes on the line*, she thought. That was unusual, since it was a nice drying day.

The front door was closed. Crista paused and peered around, hoping someone would make a noise. But all was silent. She rapped on the heavy oak door. "Nadine? Johnny? Anyone home?"

She knocked again. No sound inside.

She thought about leaving a note, but curiosity overcame her. She pushed open the door a crack and looked inside. She worried that she would find something horrible in there—two bodies with blood all over the place, or the house completely destroyed, like some monster had come down from the mountains and eaten the young couple.

But all was silent. Everything looked in place. Crista sighed and shut the door. "I wonder where they are," she said out loud.

She ambled down to the stream to see if anything lay flopping around in it, like a string of fish or some colas. She knew Johnny kept things cold there. She stooped down, stirring the chill water with her fingers. There in a small pool around the rocks were five or six fish with Johnny's white tie line through their gills and mouths. *Well, they'd been there, that was for sure. Probably went to town or something*.

There was also a six-pack of soda. Then in the distance she heard the whir of an engine. She stood and focused on it. Yes, it was the truck.

Moments later Johnny barreled into the yard. She could see Nadine lying in the truck with her head lying on the windowsill. Johnny looked worried, but he waved to Crista, then hit the brakes and turned to Nadine, talking quietly.

Nadine looked up, then put her head back on the ledge. Crista ran over to her side of the truck.

The beautiful girl's face and eyes looked gray and tired. Her skin was almost white.

"What's wrong, Johnny?"

The tall man shook his head. "I don't know. Nadine says..." He choked and looked away. Crista laid her hand on Nadine's forehead.

"She's burning up, Johnny."

"I know. I tried to help her cool off with a ride. But she says she feels terrible."

"It could be anything."

Johnny swallowed, his eyes wide with fright. "She won't go to a doctor. She says we don't have the money. I'm afraid she'll..."

Crista stared at him, then looked at Nadine. "Come on inside. She could have anything. She needs to see a doctor."

"No," Nadine suddenly wailed. "No doctors." She choked and winced in pain, then nestled down further on the seat. "Take me for another ride, Johnny. I'll be all right."

"She needs to be in bed," Crista protested.

"I know," Johnny said. "She could lose the baby."

Nadine shook her head. "I won't lose the baby. I'm all right. Just a little fever." As Crista looked closer, she noticed red splotches on her neck and arms.

Crista looked from Nadine to Johnny. She realized he felt as helpless as she did. Nadine, Crista began to realize, could be very stubborn.

Jumping out on the other side, Johnny said, "Help me get her into the cabin. I'm making her stay in bed."

Crista opened the door. Nadine nearly fell out. But Johnny sped around and they both helped her stagger into the cabin. In a few minutes Crista had her out of her woolen dress. There was a red rash all over Nadine's chest, abdomen, and legs. It looked to Crista like measles. But wasn't that a kids' disease, something you had before the age of ten? Johnny and Crista tucked her into bed. Johnny took off his red baseball cap, wiped his forehead, and sat down. "I don't know what it is. Looks like something I had when I was a kid. Measles or something."

Crista nodded. "It could be. Look, I'm going home and get a thermometer. Then I'll call my father..."

"No doctors," Nadine moaned, her arm crooked over her eyes.

"I'll just get some things," Crista said. Before they could protest, she was out of the house.

She didn't even think about the hot dogs till she had passed the spot on the trail. They were gone, but there was no sign of Rontu or any of the other dogs. But this was no time for trying to befriend the Great Dane. Nadine was sick, and it might not be measles. It might be something far worse.

· 7 ·

A Doctor's Opinion

She found the thermometer in the medicine cabinet in the little blue bathroom at the end of the aisle between the bedrooms. As she scrutinized the names of the medicines her father had set in there, she recognized several names: erythromycin, ampicillin, and Keftab, all antibiotics he had given her at different times for strep throat and swimmer's ear. But she knew she couldn't risk giving Nadine something without a doctor's approval. And she knew there was also something extremely important about not taking medicine when you were pregnant.

She grimaced, then looked in the mirror at her face. Her brown wavy hair hung almost in her eyes. She looked frightened and white. But as she looked at her face, she sucked her lower lip and said out loud, "Okay, what's the responsible thing to do?"

"Get a doctor," a voice in her head answered.

"But that might really make Nadine mad," she said again.

"So what? This could be death. And there's the baby," the voice seemed to intone.

"Okay, what's the next best thing?"

She wrinkled her face and closed her eyes, thinking. "Talk to a doctor. Find out what it might be."

That was it. Her father. She could call him.

She dashed into the kitchen and dialed her father's number. At first the nurse, Mrs. Jenson, said he was busy, but Crista insisted it was an emergency. When her father's tired voice came on, he was surprisingly patient. "Is everything all right?"

"Yes, Daddy. I need to ask you about something, though." She described Nadine's condition, saying it was a friend's.

"Someone from school?" her father said.

Crista took a deep breath. She didn't think she should reveal anything about Nadine. But what could she do? She said it. "Yes, someone from . . ." She didn't finish the sentence, hoping it wouldn't really be a lie.

Her father said, "It's very contagious. It's either German measles or an allergic reaction. If it's the first, you just have to let it wear off. If it's an allergic reaction, it could be worse. If she breaks out in hives and has a hard time breathing, she should be taken to the hospital. But it'll wear off normally in a day or so. Tell her to keep comfortable. Eat soup and tea. Lots of fluids. But don't go near her. You don't need to get German measles."

Her father suddenly laughed.

"What's so funny?" Crista was stunned he even laughed. He rarely did that.

"Oh, when I was in high school, all the girls wanted to catch it."

"How come?"

"If you get them when you're pregnant, it can cause birth defects."

Heat shot through Crista like lightning. She made a little cry, but her father didn't notice. She breathed out the words, "What kind of birth defects?"

"Blindness. Heart problems. Retardation. It's very bad for pregnant women, especially in the first few months."

An inky blackness filled Crista's mind.

Her father went on, as though describing it to a patient. "You usually only get it once. For most people it just passes. Nothing to worry about. But it sounds more like an allergic reaction to me. She probably ate something is all. Just tell her to see if it goes away by evening. If so, then it was an allergy."

Crista said, "Thanks, Daddy." When she put down the phone she was shaking. *Birth defects?*

After a few moments, trying to still her shaking and the terror that gripped her, she grabbed the thermometer, went to the pantry, and grabbed several cans of soup without even reading the labels. On the way by the library, she stopped and looked up German measles in the dictionary just so she would have an alibi for Nadine. Then she hurried out into the cool air.

What should she tell them? she wondered. No, she couldn't. There was nothing they could do. Not now. Anyway, she would question her father more about it tonight. For now she had to help Nadine get comfortable and get some soup into her so it would pass.

When she reached the cabin, Johnny paced in the living room. Nadine still lay on the bed in the bedroom, sweating and talking to herself. Crista told him what she had learned. He simply nodded. "Do you think the soup will help?"

Crista replied, "Absolutely. Don't you keep any soup up here?"

"We don't have much money," Johnny said, gazing worriedly at Nadine through the doorway. His heavy black hair lay matted against his forehead where his hat had creased it. Again Crista sensed his height. He had to be at least six-three, maybe taller.

Crista asked him to start the fire and get a pot cooking. She went into the bedroom and sat on the bed next to Nadine. "It'll be okay. I think it's an allergic reaction." *Not German measles*, she prayed in her mind. *Not that*.

Nadine didn't answer. Her face was more blotchy now than earlier, but the bumps on her flesh looked more like hives. The sweat made the bumps stand out even more. "The baby?" Nadine looked up into Crista's eyes.

Crista tried not to look upset. "It'll be all right."

"But will an allergic reaction hurt the baby? And what am I allergic to?"

Swallowing uneasily, Crista glanced at Johnny. He stood in the bedroom doorway, staring at them. Crista looked back at Nadine. "You need to think about getting well, not about that kind of thing."

But Johnny said, "What did you eat today, Nay?"

"Nothing really," Nadine said. "A pickle."

Johnny laughed and Crista smiled. "That's what all pregnant women eat," Johnny said. "What else?"

"A chocolate bar with nuts." Nadine rolled her eyes. "Want to pump my stomach?"

"Anything else?"

"A can of something."

"What?"

"Fishy stuff. It's in the trash bag. I found it in the cupboard."

Jumping up, Crista ran out of the room to the trash and looked through it. There was a shallow, aluminum can that looked like the kind sardines came in. She searched for the wrapper. Then she found it. "Smoked Oysters," it read. She shook her head with relief and exasperation, then hurried back into the room. Johnny sat on the edge of the bed, a cool washcloth on her brow.

"Smoked oysters," Crista said. "Could you be allergic to them?"

"Never had them before," Nadine answered wearily. "But they sure were good. I could go for some mo..."Suddenly she gasped and choked, then lay back.

Johnny hovered over her, and Crista watched, her heart pounding.

A moment later Nadine beamed. "That's it, fans. Oysters. I remember now. Once at Christmas we had oyster stew and I had this happen then."

Turning around, Johnny sighed noisily through his teeth. "Well, should you take anything?" He looked at Crista with frustration crossing his face. But she knew he was just relieved.

"It's my fault," Nadine said. "I should have known." Then she choked again and broke into tears. "My baby will be born sick. I know it. Everything goes wrong for us." Tears slid down her cheeks, but she stared up at the ceiling.

Crista quickly answered, "No, I don't think there's anything bad about an allergic reaction, so don't worry, okay?" She prayed she was right as she sat with Johnny on the edge of the bed. Nadine was still crying.

"I love you, Honey," Nadine said, gripping Johnny's hand. "But nothing goes right for us."

Johnny sighed, "It's going to start, Nay, so don't worry. Listen to Crista." He winked at her, then went out. A few minutes later he called, "Soup's ready." He looked like he was trying to be cheerful, but Crista could tell he was still worried.

Crista fed Nadine the soup, chicken noodle, a spoonful at a time. She took it and smiled, then patted Crista's hand. "You're a good friend," she said. "Better than lots of people I've known."

As she fed Nadine, Crista noticed again how beautiful the girl was. Then it hit her: That was what she would do—a painting of Nadine. In the doorway of the cabin. Full pregnant. She laughed to herself with joy as she pictured the scene in her mind. *I'll surprise her*, Crista thought. *Both of them.*

Soon the whole bowl had gone down, warm and toasty. When they were done, it was past six o'clock. Crista had even forgotten to show Nadine the watch. But she thought she would save that. Finally she stood up. "I have to get home. My dad'll be coming."

"I'll drive you," Johnny said.

Agreeing, Nadine took her hand. "The woods will be dangerous. Scary, anyway. Please let him take you. I feel a lot better. No more oysters for me." Already her color was coming back, and the hives and splotchy red spots had begun to disappear.

Crista began to protest, but Johnny put on his hat and grabbed the keys. "Come on, little nurse. You've still got to save all the people in town before midnight."

Smiling happily, Crista turned to Nadine, greatly relieved it wasn't German measles and no one would have to worry about birth defects. "Is it all right if I pray for you before I go?"

Nadine looked up, surprised. "Yes," she said right away. "Yes. That would be wonderful."

The bed squeaked as Crista sat down again on the edge. Nadine accepted Crista's hand, then gripped it and closed her eyes. Johnny took his hat off. She tried to think of some spiritual way to start, but nothing came to mind. She said quietly, "Lord, please protect Nadine and the baby. Let nothing bad happen to them. Thank You for having me here to help. Amen."

When she finished, Nadine looked up into Crista's eyes. "I itch all over," she said. "But that was a great prayer. Thanks."

"It'll be okay," Crista said with a confident nod. "I'm sure of it."

Nadine patted the sheet over her sweating abdomen. "Fairlight's okay too; I can feel her heart drumming away."

Chuckling, Johnny opened the door and Crista stood to go out. Nadine called after her, "Thanks again, Crista. You're a good friend."

Stopping in the doorway, she turned and winked, giving Nadine a thumbs-up. "I'm just glad I could help. I'll keep praying for you." She went out the doorway. Johnny opened the front door and then the door of the truck as Crista climbed in. He ran around the front, cranked open the handle, and jumped in. In a minute they clattered down the beaten path that went around behind the mountain and connected with the dump road. In ten minutes they were out on the highway.

Crista gave him directions. Johnny didn't say much. He kept both hands on the wheel. She showed him where the cabin road met the highway. Johnny turned, and with dust flying behind them they bumped around to Crista's house. No lights were on.

"My dad's not home yet," she commented with relief.

Johnny turned to her. "Did you ask him about the allergy?"

Grimacing, Crista stared into her lap, but then her eyes met his. She noticed how deep gray they were. She knew instantly he wasn't angry. "I had to ask my father. He's a doctor."

"I know. You told us."

She began to open the door. Johnny grabbed her hand. "It's not me that won't go to doctors," he said. He gripped it but not hard.

Crista looked him in the eyes again. "She should have one, Johnny. She should. It could be dangerous having a baby all alone up there."

"I know," Johnny said, shaking his head back and forth with frustration. "But I can't talk her out of it. She's afraid, Crista."

"But of what?"

Johnny cleared his throat. "She's an orphan, Crista. Both her parents died when she was young because of a mistake by some doctors. And she grew up in a home. She's never had a family and she's always been afraid of doctors. Always, ever since I knew her."

"But most doctors want to help," Crista insisted, her eyes suddenly filling with tears.

Johnny looked down the road. He let go of her hand and put it on the wheel. "It's for her to decide," he said. He tensed, but then turned to her. "Nadine's scared, Crista. Real scared. But she's more afraid of doctors. I've tried to persuade her. I'll get the money somehow.

But she doesn't want to owe money to anyone, and she doesn't want some doctor making something bad happen."

Crista swallowed. "You can't deliver that baby alone."

He looked away. "I know. But she's reading about it."

"You need a doctor, Johnny. You don't know what it's like up here in the winter."

He chewed his lip. "Promise me you won't tell your dad."

With a sigh, Crista bowed her head, "Okay. I promise. For now."

Johnny nodded. "Thanks. Nadine really likes you. I'm glad you came by to visit. I'm tryin' to get a job and get some health insurance. But it's tough. Anyway, so long as you don't tell anybody, we'll find a way. I promise you that. I won't let her get hurt over this."

Crista nodded and opened the door. When she shut it, Johnny tipped his hat, then hit the accelerator and sped off. She watched the dust rise as the sun began its descent toward twilight. As she stepped into the warm little cabin, she whispered, "Lord, what are we going to do?"

·8·

Allergic Reaction

"What if a lady who's pregnant has an allergic reaction, Daddy? What should she do?" Crista looked across the table that night as her father slowly ate his dinner of pork chops, peas, and applesauce. A medical journal lay open by his plate and he had been reading it. He looked up, adjusted his glasses, then turned back to the journal.

"I wouldn't worry about it," he said absently.

Crista tried to eat her peas without shaking, but they kept falling off her fork. "There wouldn't be deformities or anything?"

"Rarely," he said with a grunt. He still wasn't paying attention. But Crista thought that was probably good. She cut into a pork chop.

She waited a few minutes as their forks tinked on the plates, and each chewed a piece of meat. Her father didn't take his eyes off the journal. Crista said, "Is there anything the mother can do?"

Her father stopped and gazed at her again. "About what?"

"To prepare for having the baby?"

He looked up and a glimmer of a smile appeared on his lips. She fought back an impulse to cry "Hurrah," but he said, "Do you know someone who's pregnant?"

"Oh, I was just talking about it to some friends. We were interested." Not telling him the friends were Nadine and Johnny and letting him assume she meant school friends made her feel uneasy, but she wasn't exactly lying, so she consoled herself with that.

"There are many things a pregnant woman should be doing," her father said, putting down his knife and fork and gazing at her with bright, interested eyes. Crista remembered how at one time delivering babies was such a passion with him. She hadn't really noticed it at the time, but now it meant a lot to her that he had included his mother and her in his thoughts about being a doctor.

"She should be learning about childbirth with her husband, first of all. They should go to an obstetrician and take regular tests to assure that the baby is healthy. And she should be eating right."

"Eating right?" Crista looked up just as she was about to bite into another forkful of peas.

"Of course—a balanced diet. That's one of the most important things."

"Like eating what?"

He shook his head with wonder. "Like eating what we eat. What do you think?"

He rolled his eyes with amusement. "You sound like your mother." The moment he said it, she knew the pain had struck. He immediately turned silent, looked out the window and sighed, then started to get up, coughing. She didn't know what he was feeling, but she wished he would tell her.

But he picked up his plate and took it out to the kitchen.

She closed her eyes and pushed back a sudden burst of anger and hurt inside her breast, then turned to the window, seeing her reflection in it. Her lips were tight and drawn with anger, her eyes hard. When she saw herself looking like that she suddenly felt guilty. "Don't be that way to him," she said. "Don't treat him like that, even if you are angry."

He had filled the sink and begun doing the dishes. She picked up a towel and said hopefully, "I'll dry."

He shook his head. "My night."

"Daddy, I don't mind."

She realized he wanted to be alone, and she suddenly put down the towel. "Okay, I'll do my homework." She started down the aisle and the pegboard floor creaked under her feet. She prayed furiously that her father would stop her, but he didn't. When she reached the end of the aisle, she turned and saw his hunched shoulders in the bright kitchen lights. For a moment he looked old and frail to her, but then she realized it was the way the light fell on his neck. He was as robust as ever.

"Daddy," she said.

He turned. "Yes."

"I like helping you sometimes."

"I know," he said. "But not tonight. I'm ... I'm sorry. I just ..." He looked back at the dishwater.

"It's okay," she said. "I know you're thinking about Mom."

When he didn't answer, she walked back into the living room, cleaned off the rest of the dishes, and took them out to the kitchen. As she walked, she murmured, "I'm thinking about her too, Daddy, so don't you think we should talk about it sometime?" But he said nothing when she finally dumped the rest of the dishes into the sink.

In the living room again, she told herself to think of something else. As she sat at the table to do her homework, she began singing a song she heard on the radio. "Listen to your heart," she cooed, "when he's calling for you. Listen to your heart—there's nothin' else you can do." She sang and drew and her mood changed. Somehow it would all work out. That was what her mama had always said. "It'll all work out. So don't worry about tomorrow."

Crista visited Nadine and Johnny over the next few days. She took them homemade soup, several cans of vegetables from the home stock, and some chocolate bars she bought with her allowance. Nadine tried to refuse them, but Crista said it was just stuff they didn't really want at home. She knew Nadine realized she wasn't telling the truth, but it made it easier.

On Friday Johnny had good news: He had gotten a job in a service station. "Just taking the money when people get gas," he said with a shrug. "But it's something."

Nadine's allergic reaction was over and she felt much better. She talked about getting a job herself, but Johnny was against it. Crista didn't ask any more about it when she noticed Johnny giving Nadine a wry look.

That afternoon Crista and Nadine walked around looking for things to draw and paint. Crista's new art teacher, Mrs. Bevans, had encouraged the students to try all sorts of new forms, and Crista had some ideas.

"You have to bring it over when you're done," Nadine said as she bent down and brushed at a bit of moss on a rock. "I want to see everything." Nadine's eyes shone with admiration as she spoke. "I was never good at artwork. Everything always ended up being a picture of some movie star."

"Who?" Crista asked.

"A version of Kevin Costner," Nadine said with a giggle.

Crista laughed. "You can draw Kevin Costner?"

"Sort of. But he's the only person. I worked at it for months. Now every time I draw anyone, even a girl, they always end up looking like him. Can you imagine?"

"I think he's cute, too."

Nadine nodded. "But not cuter than Johnny."

"Right."

They both leaned down by the stream and ran their fingers in the water. Nadine pulled out a can of cola and said, "Do you want to split one?"

"I don't want to take your food, Nadine," Crista said adamantly. "And you need to eat right."

"It's only soda pop. Doesn't cost much." She threw back her blonde hair over her shoulder. Crista tried to think of some actress or model that Nadine looked like, but she couldn't think of anyone's name.

Nadine took a sip, then handed it to Crista. She gulped a long slug, then held it.

"You could be a model, I bet," Crista said.

Wrinkling her nose with mock disgust, Nadine said, "Stand around and let people photograph your figure? Forget it."

"You wouldn't like that?" Crista was astonished.

"Boring," Nadine said. "I'd rather live out in the wild, leave my hair uncombed and tote around two babies under my arms and four others trailing along behind."

Even more amazed, Crista shook her head. "You don't sound like the people I see on television."

"Aw, they're all fake. You think that's real? Real is not like that. One-liners all the time. Everyone beautiful and sexy and fun? That's not life."

Crista gazed at Nadine. For all her homey ways, she was real—that was for sure. "What do you really want to do, Nadine? I mean, really?"

As she twisted a fall of hair in her fingers, Nadine took the Coke from Crista and tilted her head back, taking a long drink. When she was done, she wiped her mouth with the back of her hand. "I'd like to lie out under the moonlight with Johnny, gaze up at the stars, and count them till I fall asleep in his arms. Then I want to wake up with him at my side and three little kids staring over the edge of the bed with big eyes at us and saying, 'You love Mommy a lot, don't you, Daddy?' And he would say 'Yes,' and then they'd look at me and say, 'You love Daddy a lot, don't you, Mommy?' And I'd say 'Yes,' and then we'd all hug and have huge pancakes with gobs of syrup for breakfast."

Crista giggled. "It does sound kind of neat."

Leaning back into the sun, Nadine suddenly plucked a bit of grass and put it between her thumbs. She blew on it and a loud screech erupted. Soon they were both blowing blades of grass, scampering around the yard, and screeching like crazed Indians. A few minutes later they made their way to the porch and collapsed into the deck chairs. Nadine patted her belly. "Johnny Junior's really beating up on me today. Or else Rebekah Fairlight is making a big batch of mudpies and winging them at the walls."

Feeling warm and happy, Crista smiled.

Nadine lay her hand on Crista's shoulder. "But I'm thinking about giving Fairlight a third name now."

"Oh, what?" Crista sat up, pushing her sneakered toe into a knothole in the porch flooring. It was past five o'clock now and the sun was moving toward sunset.

"Crista."

The moment Nadine said it, Crista gazed at her with a mixture of embarrassment and wonder.

"Really," Nadine said, squeezing Crista's shoulder. "I like that name. But especially I like you. That's why you name someone with a name like that, isn't it? Because you like the person who had it originally."

Crista swallowed and looked down at her hands. "I'd be honored," she said quietly. When she looked up, Nadine smiled.

Then she took Crista's hand. "You have a lot of hurt to deal with, don't you?"

"Not really," Crista said with a little shrug. She liked talking like this, though. She wished she could do it with her father.

Nadine looked off over the yard. "Yeah, I guess this place is quite a wreck. But it's all Johnny and I have at the moment, so we have to make the most of it." Nadine laughed. "And when you have good friends, the bad doesn't seem so bad." She let go of Crista's hand.

Sitting back, Crista basked in the warm sun peeking through the trees to the west. She knew she needed to get home. But somehow that place and that moment felt like being in the hollow of the hand of a huge giant who loved you. Crista nestled in the chair and enjoyed the warmth. Nadine was silent.

After several minutes she rose. "Guess I'd better be making Johnny's dinner. He'll be hungry. First day on the job."

Crista stood. "Yeah, I need to get home."

"And work on the drawings?"

"Yes," she said with a grin. "And make dinner. And do my homework. And hope my father will say something different..." She suddenly sighed and looked down, feeling guilty she had said that.

Nadine suddenly hugged Crista to her chest. "I love you, little sister." They held one another, then Nadine released her. "You're welcome to stay."

Crista shook her head. "No, Daddy will want dinner."

"He's a doctor?" Nadine said.

"Yes."

"Is he handsome?"

Crista had never thought about it. But now that the question had been put to her, she knew he was. Her mother had thought he was. "Yeah, he's cute, I guess."

Standing in the doorway, Nadine gazed at her thoughtfully, then said, "Someday you'll understand what he's going through."

"I know," Crista said with a nod. She pulled on her backpack. The boards on the porch creaked under her feet. A breeze riffled the treetops and licked at her cheeks. She bent into it, closing her eyes.

Nadine laughed. "That's why I like it here. That touch of wind is worth it all."

Grinning, Crista stepped off the porch. "See you next week. We're going away for the weekend. Visit some cousins."

Nadine waited in the doorway. "I'll miss you." The early moon was already coming up over the trees.

"Ever see the moon rise over the mountain at night?" she said suddenly.

Peeking through the trees, Crista spotted the misty orb. "Sort of."

"Moonlight Mountain. That's what I call it."

Crista suddenly laughed. "I've been trying to name the mountain for months. But that's it—Moonlight Mountain. That's perfect."

Nadine smiled happily. The breeze picked up and blew Nadine's hair back from her face, making her look like a beautiful model with blown dry hair. Crista started toward the woods, turning the words "Moonlight" and "Mountain" over in her mind. Then, "Fairlight of Moonlight Mountain." She laughed, and when she reached the edge of the clearing she turned and waved to Nadine, still standing on the porch. "I'll tell her later," Crista said as she bent into the growing dark.

She had left two more hot dogs at "The Love Tree" and she hoped she would cross paths with Rontu again. Maybe he would let her pet him this time. She wondered briefly if her father would let her have a dog. But abruptly she shook her head. "Not a dump dog, that's for sure. Still..."

She dared not think about it or hope. Rontu hadn't ever been particularly friendly. Who knew—maybe he preferred his freedom, hard as it was. Yet he would make a good pet. In her bones, Crista knew it. She thought maybe the next drawing she did would have a picture of a dog in it. A Great Dane. An albino Great Dane.

She laughed as she headed up the trail. Somehow the dangers of the past week seemed far away... something that only happened in books.

· 9 ·

Tricks

Crista worked hard on the drawings. She did them the first time around in charcoal. She realized they weren't that good, but anyone who knew would recognize Rontu, though she didn't plan to tell anyone.

Two weeks later she still hadn't seen Rontu, but she carted the drawings up to show Nadine. In the evening, Crista often drew on the dining room table, hoping her father would notice. One evening she thought she saw him bend over them, but then she realized he had laid a journal on the table and was reading it. He probably wouldn't say a word anyway, she thought with a flash of anger.

But she knew she couldn't stay mad at him. It did nothing, and it only made her feel bad.

At the end of September the leaves began to change to sharp reds, cool oranges, and crisp yellows. Different trees usually carried a single color. Crista made several more drawings and even some collages out of leaves. She lacquered the drawings once she finished so the colors wouldn't fade. Her father's birthday would come up in December and she wanted to do something special for him.

School moved along at a brisk pace. Arithmetic was difficult, but she had made a "half" report period of two A's, three B's, and the rest C's. For once nothing worse than a C. She hoped she could better it before the actual report period ended on October 18.

Every time she went into the woods she left something at "The Love Tree"—an extra hamburger from dinner, a blackened hot dog, a hambone. It was always gone the next time she came by. Yet she could never be sure it was actually Rontu who was finding it.

Then during the last week of September she came around the bend, planning to put down some fat cuttings from a steak they had had the night before for dinner. Rontu lay beneath The Love Tree, his right front paw casually crossed over his left paw, and his tongue dangling and floppy. When she came around the bend, he stood and barked.

Crista jumped back, then grinned. He looked friendly. Maybe it *had* been him who was scarfing up all those goodies.

Immediately she yanked off her pack and found the fat strips. She laid two on the ground in front of her. Rontu paced back and forth, then hurried forward and lapped them up, barely chewing. He looked skinnier than ever—little more than a sack of bones.

Crista cautiously dropped two more pieces directly in front of her, then edged back a few more feet. Rontu devoured them with one deft motion.

Taking out one more piece of fat, this time she placed it on the tip of her moccasin. Rontu studied it from several angles, then leaned down and chomped it off the toe with a slap of his tongue on the leather.

Feeling bolder, Crista poised the next piece of fat on her palm and bent down. "It's okay, boy. It's okay. Just take it out of my hand."

Rontu sniffed her fingers. This piece of fat had some red pieces of meat on it. She had saved the meaty bits for last. His sandpapery tongue slithered out and he jerked it off her palm with a slurp. He threw his head back and chewed, blinking his eyes with pleasure.

With only the slightest hesitation Crista reached over his head, and as his eyes popped open she touched him behind an ear. His head stood as high as her chest. Everything in the forest seemed to grow still. Rontu froze. But her hand lay trembling on his head; he didn't growl or even move away. She carefully rubbed the bony knobs above his eyes.

The huge dog blinked, then leaned up into her touch. She pressed harder. Soon she was petting him all over the head. Rontu whimpered with joy.

Crista took the two last pieces of fat and meat out of her knapsack and stepped back. She said, "Catch." She threw it underhand toward the Dane. Rontu pranced back and caught it easily in his teeth, almost sucking the bit of fat down as if starved. His tail wagged. Then Crista threw him the last piece and he caught it again. As he chewed on it, this time more scrupulously (as if to suck out all the flavor before he swallowed it), she knelt down on the ground, opened a pack of cupcakes, and fed them to him hand to mouth. He sat back on his haunches and licked her face several times, big sloppy licks that almost bowled Crista over.

When she stood up, he also rose. "Your name is Rontu. At least that's my name for you. Rontu. Hear that?"

The big Dane cocked his head. Dark brown chocolate crumbs hung from his lower jaw. Crista laughed. But she said, "Rontu. That's what I'm calling you. Come on. I want you to meet someone."

She walked off down the trail with Rontu at her side, his cropped tail wagging and his huge white body looking like that of a miniature horse. Crista rested her hand on his shoulders as they walked, feeling a bit like the little boy in *The Jungle Book* as he tamed his friends. She rubbed him on the head and behind the ears as they walked, keeping up a running monologue. "You're the first pet I ever had. Do you know who the original Rontu was? No, you couldn't know. You don't read, do you? Well, one of these days I'll read you the story. What do you like best—hot dogs, hamburgers, pork chops, or a variety? Probably a variety. You don't like to be bored, do you?" She felt so excited that she thought her heart would burst through her chestbone.

Rontu whimpered and whined with pleasure as they walked along. Crista wondered who he must have belonged to at one time. He had obviously been someone's pet, but now he had no collar. How could anyone lose a dog this big? Then she remembered how her mother often raged about people who brought dogs up to the woods and just dropped them off—like they were supposed to survive in the woods. That was how the dump dogs developed. They were all strays who had nowhere else to go. But was Rontu a stray? What if he did belong to someone and they saw him down by the road—would they want him back?

Suddenly worried about this, Crista thought more about it, then realized if Rontu's original home was nearby he probably would have found it by now. No, he was one of those throwaway dogs that some foolish person just didn't want anymore. Anyway, the joy of simply walking with him through the woods made her feel safe and powerful. She was sure Nadine would like him too.

When they reached the cabin clearing, though, Rontu would not venture beyond the edge of the trees. Crista knew she couldn't risk trying to pull him in. She stood on the edge of the woods wondering what to do. Nadine wasn't out back or outside at all. She finally decided to let him sit while she found Nadine.

She turned to the big dog as he whined and craned his neck back and forth, looking back at the woods. "Okay, you stay here, all right? You just stand here. I want you to meet someone." She waited till he faced her. Then she repeated the words quietly. Rontu obviously didn't like being near the house. Had Johnny ever scared him away or anything? Crista wondered. She couldn't remember him saying anything about it, though he had mentioned seeing the Great Dane.

She gazed into his cool blue eyes rimmed with reddish eyelids. Rontu wouldn't look her in the eye and his eyelids kept flickering about. She noticed that his haunch was trembling. "You'll stay here, won't you? You won't run away?"

He turned and gazed back at the woods. She realized he was probably more afraid of them than they were of him. The thought struck her as funny, and she chuckled, then bent down and hugged him. "It's all right. I know you're scared. But don't be. I'll be with you."

He threw his head back as if he started to nod, then woofed loudly.

"That's right. Courage!" She patted his head. "Okay, you wait here. If you're not here when I come back, I'll just have to meet you again in the woods. But Nadine is my best friend and I really want her to meet you."

Lolling out his tongue, Rontu sat back on his haunches, then scratched his ribs with his monstrous right foot. His head came up to her chest. She figured that foot could probably swat down an elephant if it wanted to.

With an affectionate chuckle and final caress over his ears, Crista turned and hurried over to the cabin. When she knocked on the door, Nadine's voice answered from within. "Johnny?"

"It's Crista." She pushed open the door.

Nadine sat at the table reading. Crista recognized it as a baby book.

"I met him."

The cabin air was warm with the smell of vegetable soup. A fire barked and spit in the fireplace. Nadine looked up and put the book facedown on the table. "Mr. Wonderful?"

"Rontu. The Great Dane. The big white one."

Immediately Nadine's eyes lit. "Just now?"

"He's right outside. Do you want to see him?"

She jumped up. "Sure! You don't think he'll run away? I'm pretty scary with this huge stomach." She patted the bulge behind her dress.

Crista laughed. "I don't know. Let's look."

They stepped out into the cool October air. The mountain swelled with rich breezes carrying the lively fragrance of pine boughs. The trees around the clearing were aflame with red, gold, yellow, and orange, as if a painter had flung his pallette into the air and it landed there.

The big Dane stood panting and tall on the edge of the clearing.

"He's still there," Crista whispered. "I'm afraid he might run away."

"I'm not that bad, am I?" Nadine said gaily and giggled girlishly.

Crista led her slowly across the clearing. "He seems real tame. He let me pet him and everything. But I think he's afraid of the houses. Maybe he's had some bad experiences."

"Undoubtedly. Even Johnny isn't a dog lover."

They sauntered casually toward Rontu, trying not to appear threatening. Rontu whined and turned to the woods twice, but in the end he let Nadine and Crista walk all the way up to him. Crista pet his head and soon Nadine had given him a hug. Crista showed her how he had caught the meat, except this time she used a stick. Rontu retrieved it several times. But he still wouldn't step into the clearing.

They talked and played with the dog for a few minutes. "I bet I can teach him some tricks," Crista suddenly said.

"He might even know some already," Nadine added.

"Well, let's see, I have some more cupcakes." Crista set her backpack down and rifled through until she touched the cellophane packets.

"All right, sit, Rontu."

The dog eyed her with a spunky look in his eyes, then slowly sat back on his backside, reared his great head back, and woofed throatily.

"He does know some things," Nadine cried, clapping her hands. Crista flipped him a half cupcake and he wolfed it down.

"How about 'down'? Do you know how to do down?" Crista said.

The dog's eyes flickered and he looked away, as if not understanding.

Crista quickly changed the command. "Lie down. Can you lie down?"

The dog woofed, then sank to his chest, crossing his legs and looking for all the world like a rich man in his evening jacket smoking a pipe. Crista and Nadine laughed heartily as Crista threw him another cupcake.

"Play dead," Crista suddenly said. "Play dead."

The dog obviously understood the game now and had clearly been trained well by someone. He fell to his side, raised his legs slightly into the air, closed his eyes, and was still.

Both girls clapped their hands. "Wonderful!" Crista cried. As Rontu jumped back to his feet, she gave him another piece of cupcake, this time on her palm. "He's a genius!" Crista said. "I've run into the dump dog genius!"

With a giggle Nadine said, "How about roll? You think he knows that?"

"Let's try it. Roll, Rontu. Can you roll?"

The dog whined unhappily and cocked his head. He stared hard at them, but did nothing.

"Rock and roll," Nadine said with a chuckle.

Crista wrinkled her forehead. "Let's see—somersault, would that be it? Somersault!" The dog still didn't move. "How about flip? Do you know flip?"

Still the dog gazed at them quizzically.

"Maybe he doesn't know that one," Crista said sadly.

"Speak!" Nadine suddenly said. Rontu instantly woofed loudly and Crista threw him another piece of the delectable cupcakes.

"I know he knows it," Crista suddenly said. "I bet he does. We just haven't hit on the right wording. What could it be?"

"When you roll, you go all the way over."

Rontu barked suddenly.

"Over?" Crista said questioningly. "Is it 'over'?"

Immediately Rontu buckled to his chest and in a gallant legs-over-back he rolled majestically, coming up on his feet and leaping with joy. Crista threw him the last cupcake and clapped wildly. "He's great! He's so great!"

Nadine hugged her and they both hugged Rontu happily.

Suddenly glancing at her watch, though, Crista decided she had to get home, so she and Rontu left Nadine at the edge of the woods. They headed back up the trail. Rontu followed her all the way to the road. But when a car whooshed by, he stopped and turned to go up the trail.

Crista called after him. "Rontu! Rontu!"

He looked back sadly. Then he seemed to nod his head and stepped off into the woods. Crista shouted, "I'll be back tomorrow. I promise. I'll bring you some goodies. Some hot dogs."

She heard his feet shuffling through the rubbery fall leaves. He disappeared behind some rocks, and a few minutes later Crista stood alone on the edge of the highway. The late afternoon sun would soon be setting.

Crista chewed her lip. "Lord, please let him come back," she whispered. "Let him be all right."

She crossed the highway and hurried home, resolving to bring the hot dogs in rolls with ketchup and mustard.

·10·

A Friend in Need

Through October, Crista met Rontu in the woods regularly. He usually waited for her at The Love Tree. She began teaching him more tricks. Beyond the tricks he had proved he already knew, she discovered he could shake paws (the command was "paw") and retrieve (the expression was "go get it"), and leap, in which he leaped into the air to catch something she threw. But she also taught him to catch a Frisbee, heel, dig, and dance. Dance was the most difficult, but soon he was prancing in place, looking more like a middle linebacker on a football team than a ballet dancer pirouetting. But it was fun. Try as she might, though, she could not get him to go near the houses, even Nadine's, though he would stay at the edge of the clearing.

Nadine continued to get bigger and bigger. Her outsize dresses couldn't conceal her billowing belly. But she was proud and let Crista touch it to feel the baby's heart beating. Even through the cloth and flesh, Crista felt the bump bump of the stout little heart. Her belly felt rather lumpy, but Crista said, "It's really in there." In her mind, though, she prayed, "Please,

Lord, let it be healthy. That's all I ask." Frequently she and Nadine prayed together about it, and Crista discovered that her friend knew a lot about Christian faith and had believed as a young girl herself.

In late October shortly before Halloween, Crista hopped off the bus to turn down the cabin road. She planned to leave her books and head into the woods. The bus roared off, leaving a billow of acrid black smoke behind it. Then a sharp bark from the other side startled her.

She peered across the road and there stood Rontu. He jerked his head twice, then barked again, a deep, mellow woof. But it was a bark of distress, not greeting.

"Rontu! What's wrong?" Crista looked both ways, then sprinted across the road. Before she reached the other side, Rontu whipped around and bounded up the trail, his huge paws clapping on the packed, rocky path.

"What is it?" Crista shouted again as she ran after him. He barked, stopped, waited a moment, then bounded off again before she reached him. It was all uphill and Rontu nearly galloped. In a few minutes Crista puffed with exhaustion.

"Rontu, please!" Her side ached and the pack on her back felt sweaty and heavy. But the dog didn't let up.

He passed Elbow Rock and then The Love Tree. As they came around a bend, he slowed enough to let Crista catch up. When she reached him, she grabbed the skin around his neck.

"Slow down! I'm not a deer, you know." She breathed hard and panted. Rontu stopped, looked at her, and waited. But he was restless and whimpered repeatedly. She bent down and looked into his eyes. "What's wrong? Is it Nadine and Johnny?"

Rontu turned again up the trail. But a few yards up he suddenly veered off into the woods, barking loudly. It was not in the direction of the Semms' house, so Crista breathed a prayer of thanks that whatever it was probably did not involve them.

The dog sped ahead through the underbrush, over rocks, around trees. He barked repeatedly and soon Crista heard a response. She slowed down. Were there other dogs—other dump dogs around? Surely Rontu wouldn't lead her into a pack of them.

Then she saw it. A little collie-like dog, maybe a shelty. By a tree. Pulling at something.

As she moved closer, cautiously, Rontu stopped. He looked back and forth from the shelty to her, as if pointing it out. "See? Look at this. We need your help."

Crista knelt and looked at the little dog. It was missing one eye, with a jagged, painful-looking gash where a deep brown eye should have been. The moment it saw her, it began growling. As she edged closer, the dog jerked its paw back. A trap. It was caught in a trap.

Its right foot was bleeding, the flesh cut and bleeding in the teeth of the trap.

As she worked to get closer she held out her hand. "It's all right. It'll be all right. Just calm down." The dog growled, then whimpered. The trap was chained to a stake. She knew trappers came to these woods trying to get fox, rabbits, and squirrels. But it was a larger trap. Was someone trying to get dump dogs?

Instantly she was angry. The poor dog was caught in a rusty, ugly trap. It looked strong, too. She wasn't sure she could pull the jaws apart. She opened her pack to see if she had anything left from lunch. But there was only an apple core. Dogs didn't usually like fruit.

She spoke low and kindly, trying to calm the little shelty. But as she reached out to touch the trap, the dog bared its fangs, revealing black angry lips tinged with froth and short, spiky fangs. She knew if she got too close it might charge her. Rontu barked. But obviously he couldn't help her with this.

She knew she needed someone else to help. Once she had read in a book how someone had freed a fox from a trap, so she thought she knew how they could do it. But she needed some food, a blanket, and a friend.

"Johnny," she whispered.

The dog stopped growling, but when she stood it bared its teeth again. "Okay," Crista said. "You stay here, Rontu. Protect him. I'll get Nadine. Or Johnny."

Rontu seemed to understand. When she pulled her pack back on and hurried back to the trail, he watched her but did not move. Crista thought maybe the two dogs were friends. But that eye? How pitiful.

She found Nadine and Johnny both at home when she ran breathless into their clearing. Nadine was already big and bulging, but she wanted to come. They brought an old blanket from the shed and some rolls from lunch. All three hurried through the woods to where the dogs were. When Rontu saw them, he bounded up to Crista and then Nadine, giving each a friendly lick as if to apologize for the shelty's poor manners.

The dog remained just as terrified and vicious as before. Crista spelled out her plan. Johnny volunteered to throw the blanket, while Nadine and Crista would pull apart the trap.

Crista crept closer to the dog while Johnny went around behind him with the blanket. She dropped the roll in front of the dog. It remained wary of Johnny, but after it sniffed the roll, it bent down to take a bite. Crista smiled to herself, thinking, Even when they're in pain they still like to eat.

The dog took the roll as Rontu watched with large, blue, attentive eyes. Johnny moved closer. He threw the blanket. It sailed down over the dog's back and head. Johnny jumped quickly. He pulled the bottom of the blanket over the dog's head and clamped it down. The dog squirmed and growled, but the blanket protected Johnny from his teeth.

"Do it!" Johnny yelled.

Crista grabbed the jaws of the trap in her hands and Nadine pushed down the latch. The jaws came apart and the dog jerked its leg up. Johnny picked him up still in the blanket, then set him down easily. Everyone stood back as the dog squirmed and squealed. Then Johnny let him go.

Instantly the dog worked his way out of the blanket, then scorched a three-legged gallop through the trees. Rontu exploded after him and caught up in a few bounds. Both dogs stopped in the woods about 40 feet from Crista and the Semms. Rontu's tail wagged and the little shelty held up its paw, panting. Rontu bent down and licked it. Then he turned his head toward Crista, Johnny, and Nadine and shook it up and down, barking.

"He's saying thank you," Crista whispered, her eyes filling with tears at the thought of the poor little dog. Would his leg ever be good again?

The shelty held its bloody paw up gingerly. Rontu trotted over to the group, turned around, and waited.

He sat, scratched his haunches, and moved his head several times. The dog stood looking at them with its one eye.

"Not exactly a show winner, I'd say," Johnny commented.

"Well, at least he's out of that wretched trap," Nadine said. She put her arm around Crista's shoulders. "We're going to call you Florence Nightingale."

Crista smiled. Nadine's warmth felt good and friendly. "I knew I couldn't just leave him there," Crista answered.

"Of course not. But he can't just roam around in the woods either," Johnny said, wiping his forehead. He wore a denim jacket and jeans.

"We can't make him come with us," Nadine replied. "Even Rontu won't come near the house."

They waited. Rontu walked back and forth between them and the shelty several times. But the little dog wouldn't come closer.

Nadine said, "Well, what are you going to name this one?"

"Tigger," Crista said, using the first word that came into her mind as she looked at the poor little creature. "He's a fighter and he's cute like Tigger in the Pooh books."

Johnny laughed. "Maybe he and Rontu live together. They must be friends or something."

"I'll bring them both something each time I come into the woods," Crista said finally.

Nadine turned. Johnny put his arm over her shoulder and they began walking back toward the trail. Crista watched Tigger as Rontu gave him another lick on the foot. The huge Dane and the shelty looked like a real pair of ruffians, she thought with a smile. She called to them, "Stay out of the traps, you guys. We don't want to find your bones one of these days rotted away."

Sitting on his haunches, Rontu threw his head back, dribbling out his tongue and woofing happily. Tigger gazed up at him, looking like a toddler who didn't understand the joke.

Crista laughed. "I'll be back," she said.

She caught up to Nadine and Johnny as they reached the trail. "I'd better get this stuff home," she said. "I haven't even dumped my books off."

"Do you want to come up for a cola?" Nadine said with a smile. She looked like she had trouble walking, but Crista wouldn't say anything about that.

"I'll have to see how things look first at home. Thanks for helping."

"Anytime," Johnny said. "We're the local dump dog ambulance service."

Crista chuckled. Nadine hugged her. The protruding belly felt hard and taut. "I'll bet you were scared," she said.

"But it makes you feel good," Crista said, gathering up her things.

Nadine let go of her and stepped back, putting her arm around Johnny's waist. Johnny gave her a quick kiss and she looked up at him, then pulled the bill of his hat down over his eyes. Crista and Nadine laughed. Johnny pushed the hat onto the back of his head and rolled his eyes wryly. The blanket was draped over his arm. Nadine smiled proudly at him and Crista turned away, remembering how her mother had looked into her eyes like that. A breeze fluttered the leaves overhead and a squirrel suddenly skittered across the path below them.

As she hurried down the path toward home, Crista waved, then turned a corner and waved again. She watched as they headed up the path toward the cabin. As she walked, she worried about the two dogs. But she was sure they would be all right now. "Just don't let them get into any more traps," she said out loud as she passed Elbow Rock.

On the way down she decided she did have time to come back and bring some food for the dogs. She wondered if Tigger would also become friendly like Rontu had. She hoped he would, then sighed as she sprinted across the highway.

"I wish I could tell Daddy about all this," she murmured as she reached the other side. But somehow that seemed impossible. He had already referred to them as dump dogs and mongrels. He would never let her have one of them as a pet.

·11·

Trick or Treat

On Halloween Crista dressed up as an artist with a beret, a painting palette, several brushes, a multi-blotched smock, a painting she was working on, and an easel. Before she rang a bell or knocked, she set up the easel and posed, then pointed to the words "Trick or Treat" at the bottom of the painting. Over it was a picture of Rontu in the middle with Tigger next to him and Nadine and Johnny behind them.

It was a fair likeness. Crista was a talented artist. She had recently discovered acrylic painting in the art classes which the school offered in early October under Mrs. Bevans. But while everyone else passed on to other forms—sculpture and watercolors—Crista continued to work at home with the acrylics that Mrs. Bevans gave her.

Even though the dogs and people would not be easily recognizable to anyone who knew them, she was getting better at it every day. She practiced in the evenings, doing still lifes of cups, fruit, and tables in the house. She also worked on a portrait of her father lying back in his green recliner chair smoking his pipe and reading. She planned to give it to him for his birthday, December 2.

Crista wasn't sure whether she should go by Nadine and Johnny's for trick or treating. They hadn't said anything about it. But she felt afraid they might be offended if she didn't. She decided to go after she had walked both streets end to end in her own community.

She carried the easel in her left hand with the big Eveready flashlight her father kept in the closet. She gripped the painting, brushes, and palette with her other hand. She took the candy and goodies in her backpack. It would be a long hike, she knew, but she felt excited and expectant. If nothing else, she and Nadine would simply talk.

The steep trail bent into the trees and her breath came hard. She watched for signs of Rontu and Tigger, but they didn't seem to be around. She knew candy wasn't good for dogs, but Mrs. Krump down the street had given her two popcorn balls and she thought she could feed that to them.

She rounded the bend and flashed the light ahead to the tree, her heart suddenly hammering. Rontu was there. He jumped up. Then she saw Tigger too. He sprang into the bushes a moment, then nosed his little brown-and-white face out from behind one as Rontu bounded down toward her barking. In a moment he spewed hot breath and a sloppy tongue all over her face. She nearly dropped the pallette and everything else.

"Trick or Treat," she exclaimed to Rontu as he pranced around her in his ungainly, long-legged way. He woofed lightly. He was obviously happy to see her.

With Rontu leaping and woofing, Crista easily found the popcorn balls. She tore off the paper as Rontu whined with delight.

Tigger trotted warily at the edge of the trail, still favoring the front paw that had been caught in the trap. As Rontu chewed the popcorn ball, Crista knelt down low to the ground. "Come here, Tigger. It's all right. I have something for you."

The dog whimpered and wheeled back and forth, but he kept drawing closer. Crista broke off a chunk of the other half-ball and pitched it toward the smaller dog. Rontu watched, but continued gnawing on the caramel-laced half-ball. Tigger hurried back and forth, his back bristling slightly. Finally he lapped up the chunk, chewing and swallowing it quickly.

Crista threw him another.

He pounced on it and scarfed it up heartily.

Finally she had fed both dogs the two balls. Then she said, "I'm going to Nadine's. Want to follow me over?" She picked up the easel, painting, and other materials. "Well, if you want to come, you'll have to be friendly. As you know, Nadine's going to have a baby. She doesn't want any dog nosing up her skirt. Hear, Rontu?"

His eyes had that sad, drowsy Great Dane look. She didn't think he really understood anything. But it felt good to talk to them. She marched brightly up the path, the flashlight weaving back and forth in front of her. With Rontu and Tigger she felt safer and more confident. The big Dane joined her and kept pace at her side. Tigger growled, then followed 20 feet behind.

When she reached the clearing, neither dog would go any further. Crista hurried across the clearing, trying to be quiet. She wanted to surprise them.

Crista heard voices, though, and as she set up her easel at the door, it suddenly burst open. Two people in horrible werewolf masks leaped out at her. Crista jumped back with a shriek, tripping over the easel. Rontu roared from the other side of the clearing and came bounding toward them.

Johnny ripped off his mask and let out a raucous laugh. Nadine pulled off hers as Rontu barked at them furiously behind Crista. But she patted him on his head and quieted him.

Slapping his leg, Johnny cried, "I knew there was some way to get that dog into the yard."

Nadine laughed. "We were hoping you'd come. We've been on the lookout all afternoon. We have a surprise."

Rontu paced back and forth in front of the cabin, sniffing the edge of the porch. Then, sure that all was well, he trotted back to the edge of the clearing.

"Oh, not good enough for you, huh!" Johnny called, pulling the mask back on. He roared again, but Rontu just lay down and nipped at his back leg. Tigger sat down beside him.

Nadine threw her arm around Crista. "So what have you got here? Is this your Halloween outfit?"

It was bright in the lights at the front of the cabin. Johnny had brought out two gas lamps and set them on the porch. Crista showed them the whole getup.

Nadine stepped back and gazed at the painting. "That's us," she said with a hoarse, amazed whisper.

Crista felt herself blush. "I tried."

As Nadine bent closer, she whistled. "It really is good. In fact, incredible. How do you do it? Look at this, Johnny."

Dropping his mask onto the porch, Johnny knelt down by the painting. "You even put my red baseball cap on," he said. "I didn't know I was that handsome."

Nadine gave him a little shove. Her big belly pushed her dress out as she stood, pulling back her long blonde waves. She gave Crista a wink. "There's something missing, though." She squinted at Crista, then smiled craftily. "I know." She disappeared into the cabin, then came back out with a piece of charcoal and her hand mirror. She motioned to Crista to come close.

"What you need is a little French mustache," Nadine said, grinning crazily.

Crista bent forward and Nadine drew two arms of a curly mustache under her nose. Then she held up the mirror. Crista laughed and bowed. "Ah, mademoiselle. You want a bootiful picture for yerzelf and your oosband?"

Nadine clapped her hands together. "Perfect! All right, come on in for the surprise."

Looking off across the clearing to Rontu and Tigger, she smiled as both dogs continued sitting up, watching everything going on with wide eyes. She waved to them, then stepped into the house.

On the table was a big chocolate cake on it with candles all over the top. They were lit.

"It's not my birthday," Crista exclaimed.

"But it's Johnny's," Nadine said, giving Johnny a quick hug. His face reddened.

"You didn't tell me," Crista said. "I would have gotten..."

Nadine waved her away. "Being here is present enough. Now Johnny, blow out the candles so we can see if this cake tastes any good."

The cabin smelled of lilac and chocolate and it was warm inside, like an embrace from a favorite aunt. Johnny leaned over and blew out all the candles. Nadine quickly produced a present, a bright new green Philadelphia Eagles coach's cap. He pulled it on and grinned toothily.

"He's 20 today," Nadine said to Crista. "A fifth of a century."

Johnny grimaced. "You don't have to make it sound so old."

As they kissed, Crista went outside and brought in the painting. "Then the least I can do is give you a present. Would you like this? It's not quite finished. But I could come out and do the rest next week."

Nadine picked it up and stood it on the ledge over the fireplace "We'll hang it up later. That's wonderful." She gave Crista a hug.

As they ate the moist chocolate cake, Nadine explained that Johnny had figured out how to operate the gas stove. "We had the butane bottle filled in town and hooked it up. Now we can use the stove all the time. And there's an electric generator in the shed. If we can get it running, we can actually have electricity." Nadine looked at Johnny with obvious pride in her eyes.

As Nadine talked, Crista remembered how it had been when her mother was alive. She was always having surprise parties and making up fun things to do. Suddenly the deep pain of the memory filled her as she looked around at the happy faces. She fought to hold back the tears. But Nadine kept up a happy chatter, not noticing Crista's sudden change. *Your fault*, she told herself. *If not for you, she might be here right now*. She choked on a bite and coughed.

Nadine looked at her, alarmed. "Is it that bad?"

Crista shook her head. She realized Nadine was probably the best friend she had ever had. Except for her mother.

Tears burned into her eyes again. She wasn't even sure why. When she looked up, Nadine and Johnny were both gazing at her.

"Is something wrong, Crista?" Nadine put her fork down.

"It's okay."

Nadine shook her head. "Is your father talking to you about things at all?"

Crista sighed, calming her emotion. "He's very busy."

"Busy my eye."

Swallowing back the sudden pain, Crista looked down at the cake. "It's good cake. Maybe Rontu and Tigger would like a piece."

"Sure," Nadine said, getting up. She kept looking across the room at Crista with obvious concern.

Crista didn't even know why she had been so emotional. It came at her suddenly like that at times, usually when she was having a good time with someone. She didn't like it, but it was as though her mother just popped out everywhere she turned. Her mother brushing her long reddish-blonde hair. The accident. Her mother lying crumpled in the street.

Then the feeling would be gone and she would be all right.

Nadine sat down with the pieces of cake on two chipped and cracked blue plates. Crista rose and picked them up. "I'll take them to the dogs."

Nadine stood with her. "I'll go with you. Johnny, could you pump out a bucket of water?"

As they walked Nadine said, "I bet you'd really like to have Rontu and Tigger as your own."

Shrugging, Crista sighed. "It would be nice. Or some pet, anyway. But my father would never . . . he never liked dogs. Mom wanted to have one once, but he said he wasn't ready for that."

"Maybe they could stay here. I'd take care of them for awhile. At least they wouldn't be out roaming in the woods all the time. They could sleep in the shed—if they'd come onto the property."

Tigger was already backing into the trees as the two girls approached. But Rontu hurried forward to greet them. Crista set down the plate in front of Rontu, then placed the second one a few feet away. She called to Tigger.

The small shelty didn't move.

Nadine said, "Give him time."

They both waited, without speaking. As if to meld in with the scenery, both Nadine and Crista stood perfectly still about ten feet from the plates. Tigger whimpered, then crept forward one hesitant step at a time. Rontu had already scarfed down his piece. But he seemed to know the other piece was for his friend. He turned to watch what Tigger was doing. Finally he barked with encouragement.

Still fighting his fears, Tigger finally edged up to the plate, dragged off the piece of cake, and ate it off the ground. But he didn't run back into the woods.

Nadine took Crista's hand. "I'll bet we could keep them here for the winter. They'd be awful cold, but I bet we could get them to stay. You could, anyway."

As Nadine's warm hand enclosed hers, Crista realized how much she liked the touch. It also reminded her of her mother, but in a good way. The grieving feelings of a few minutes ago were gone.

"I could bring some blankets from home and stuff," Crista said. "You don't think Johnny would mind?"

"He always does whatever I want," Nadine said with a little shake of her head.

Stifling a chuckle, Crista turned back to the two dogs.

Nadine suddenly poked her in the ribs. "Hey, that's the way it's supposed to be, isn't it?"

"I guess I'll find out someday."

After the dogs finished, Nadine picked up the plates and led Crista back over to the cabin. Rontu and Tigger kept their distance, sniffing and pacing back and forth. But they appeared interested.

The flashlight shining on the path ahead, Nadine opened the creaky metal door of the shed. It was made out of gray sheet metal, rusted on the outside in places. The door squeaked and bucked as Nadine pushed at it. But finally it slid all the way open. Inside was a lawnmower and some shelves with tools, flowerpots, cookware, and other things on them. A rake, shovel, pick, and axe hung diagonally on the right wall. The floor was dirt with several weeds growing in the middle. Crista noticed the big generator in the back on the right side.

"We could put the blankets right here in the middle," Nadine said, directing the light to the spot. She dipped her head and stepped inside. "If it was real cold, I guess we could let them inside the cabin."

Crista breathed out loudly. The air in the shed was dense, as if sopped with someone's sweat. "It kind of smells."

"That'll go away if we air it out each day. What do you think?" Nadine arched her eyebrows confidently. "All we have to do now is convince them it's the smart thing to do."

The two dogs lay in the yard now, biting and nipping at their flanks.

"And get them a flea bath," Crista said. "I bet whole families of fleas inhabit their backs."

Nadine laughed musically. They stepped out of the shed and closed the doors. Then they went back into the cabin, leaving the two dogs still sitting in the backyard. Johnny came in with the bucket of water and sloshed it into the sink. Nadine told him about her plan. He just grunted, "Anything you want, Nay."

Nadine gave Crista a quick wink.

A little later they tried to coax the dogs into walking more comfortably about on the property, but both remained shy. Nadine suggested that if they worked with them each day, maybe they would feel safe eventually.

"Winter will be hard," Nadine added. "I just hope they're not going to be stubborn about it."

"You really will stay here for the winter?" Crista suddenly said, for the first time thinking of the baby.

Nadine nodded absently. "I think it'll be beautiful."

"And cold."

The older girl shrugged. "Johnny's been cutting wood. We found a chainsaw in the shed and he got it running. Did you see the pile?" She motioned behind the house and Crista remembered seeing the beginnings of a large pile. But it would take a lot of wood to heat the cabin all winter. And what if they were snowed in? And what about having the baby?

Sighing heavily, Crista was afraid to ask Nadine about it. She didn't want a disagreement. But deep down she wondered if they really knew what it was like having a baby in a cabin—without a doctor.

How could Nadine be so sensible about the dogs and so stubborn about having a baby in a cabin in the woods? But she already knew the answer. She remembered how Johnny had told her about Nadine's fear of doctors. Still, she knew her dad was a good doctor and wouldn't make any mistakes.

Crista pushed the thoughts out of her mind. For now all she could do was try to persuade them to get a doctor and have the baby in the local hospital. But she had no idea how she could do it, or where to start. She had been praying every night before bed, but again she shot up another prayer silently. "Please, God, make it all work out."

As she spoke it, she suddenly smiled. A baby! Nadine was having a baby. That was the important thing. And it would be healthy. And it would be happy. It would have two lovely, loving parents. And if it was a girl, she would be named Rebekah Fairlight Crista Semms.

Suddenly Crista realized that Johnny and Nadine were gazing at her wonderingly. With a leap she hugged them both. "I really love you guys," she said.

Nadine patted her back. "We love you too, Crista."

A moment later both dogs barked, and they looked out the front door. The two of them stood there, gazing in at the threesome and wagging their tails.

"Probably want the main course," Nadine said, "now that they've had dessert."

Everyone laughed and went outside to hug the dogs and give them some scraps.

·12·

The Question

Several days later on a Sunday afternoon, Crista and her father worked in the yard raking the brown leaves of fall into big black plastic bags. Her father smoked his pipe. The leaves rustled as he swept them into piles with the wide, green-tined rake. They both worked in silence. It was a job they did together each fall before winter.

In front of Crista's house were several huge rocks that bordered the parking area. The siding of the cabin was stained with redwood. Crista knew her father could have afforded a mansion, but he liked the ease of country life.

As they gathered the leaves into piles, Crista suddenly said, "Would you like me to get some drinks? I'm hot." For early November it was a bit muggy.

Her father nodded, blew a cloud of smoke into the air, and took his pipe out of his mouth. He tapped out some ashes on the heel of his boot, then stuck it back between his teeth. He wore a light windbreaker and his tousled brown hair riffled in the wind. Crista noticed again that he was a handsome man. She wondered what it was that made him so silent, so cheerless. But he said nothing, and she went to the door without looking back. He followed her inside.

Crista threw off her denim jacket and the hiking boots and shuffled in her socks out to the kitchen. "Do you want a soda?"

"Cherry'll do."

When they sat down at the table looking at their drinks, her father gazed out the picture window toward the lake. His thoughts seemed far away. Crista had other reasons for bringing him inside. She knew raking leaves and working in the yard usually put him into a good mood. She wanted to ask him some questions.

The day before Nadine had been complaining about pains, and Crista wanted to know what happened when a baby was ready to come. But she still felt she couldn't reveal to her father about Johnny and Nadine.

She sipped slowly at the Coke, letting the biting bubbles catch in her throat. "The leaves are deep this year."

Her father grunted and sucked on his pipe. "No different from last year." He blinked and yawned and glanced uneasily at Crista several times. Why was it so hard to talk to him?

"The lake will freeze soon, too."

He nodded. She thought he was watching some chipmunks play on the slate patio below the big window. She fixed her eyes on them. The black and white stripes down their backs rippled as they scurried back and forth biting and chirping. Once, four years ago, she had caught one in a trap. She hid some peanuts under a huge empty four-gallon paint can, then propped it up with a clothespin and tied a string around the pin. When the "chippie" darted underneath to grab one of the nuts, she jerked the line. The can came down over him. He was caught.

She hadn't thought to put a tray or flat piece of cardboard under the paint can to make moving the catch easily. Instead, she had to slide one under afterward. In the process the poor little chipmunk got caught and died, probably of a heart attack.

When she had finally dropped him into a jar for safekeeping, he was dead. She cried off and on for two days, feeling like a murderer. She resolved never to try to catch an animal against its will after that. That was how she felt about Rontu and Tigger too. If they didn't want to be her pets, she wouldn't force them.

Her father said nothing as he smoked and drank his cherry cola. Out of the corner of her eye she studied his face. The bristly brown mustache and long lanky hair made him look like a reformed hippie, the kind she had seen in movies on TV. But his brown eyes were gentle. Even with his seeming inability to talk to her, she knew he was a gentle man. That was what her mother had said. "When you get married, look for someone gentle like your father."

Crista worked up her courage, but she couldn't think of an easy way of starting a conversation. She decided to try a completely different route. "Did you ever have a pet when you were a boy, Daddy?"

He took a swig of his cola and set down his pipe. Still gazing out the window, he said, "We had lots of them. I lived on a farm."

She knew that. She knew he had lots of pets. She knew he knew. But what could she say?

"Can you tell me about them?" She tried to sound casual, like it was normal between them to talk like this.

He shrugged. "There's nothing to tell. They lived. They died. That's it."

"Didn't you ever have a special one?"

He turned and looked at her, then gazed back out the window. He picked up the pipe. "Oh, I guess a little dog. Junior, we called him. A mutt. I took him fishing. He followed me to school sometimes."

"When did you have him?"

He scratched his hair and touched his mustache, a movement she had seen often. "He died when I was 13."

Crista took a deep breath as silently as she could. "Were you sad?"

He turned and pushed his chair back from the table. "Yes, I guess I was sad." He glanced at her nervously. Then he said, "Crissy, I know you don't understand things about me. I'm sorry. But I feel all bottled up now. I know..." His voice trailed off and he coughed. "I know I shouldn't be so silent around here. But I just feel empty inside. Ever since..." He coughed again and cleared his throat. "Please, Honey, ask me anything you want. But sometimes I just can't talk. Can you live with that?"

He blinked at her unhappily and suddenly she wanted to run to him and hug him. But she sat there without moving, feeling stunned and uncertain. Then she said, "Daddy, I understand, I think."

He nodded and sighed, then said, "We'd better finish that leaf work."

Crista picked up her cola can, still three-quarters full. She called to him as he walked toward the door, "Would you ever let me have a pet, Daddy?"

He didn't seem to hear her. He brushed ashes off the back of his hand into his palm and dumped them into an ashtray on the table by the couch.

"Do you think I could ever have a pet, Daddy?"

He wiped off his hands on his pants and turned around. "Someday, I suppose. I don't see why not." Then he started out the door.

Crista called, "If I wanted one now, would you let me?"

He was already out the door.

Crista bit her lip and shook the cola angrily. It foamed and a few drops shot out onto her wrist and the table. She ran into the kitchen, dumped out the rest, then threw the aluminum can into the bag underneath the sink. She walked out to the front door telling herself just to be calm, then pulled on her boots and her denim jacket. Her father had begun raking leaves again, and streams of blue smoke rose from his pipe in a feathery spiral.

Gritting her teeth, Crista walked over to him. She was going to make him talk about this whether he liked it or not. "Daddy, I asked you if you'd let me have a pet now if I wanted one."

He didn't even look at her. "Probably not," he said. His rake scraped on the dirt.

"Why not?"

"Because we don't need more problems than we already have."

"What problems do we have?" Crista's hands were on her hips. She chewed her lip and worked at keeping herself from yelling at him.

"I don't know," her father said, his voice a still monotone. "We have to get these leaves done, that's the first problem. I don't really want to discuss this."

Crista decided she wasn't going to give up. Not now that she'd started. "Well then, when can we?"

He sighed. "When can we what?"

"Discuss it."

"Not now."

"When?"

"Not now. Let's get these leaves done." He looked at her with frustration, a twitch of pain on his lips. "Crissy, if you want a pet, I'll think about it. What kind of pet would you want?" He sighed as if he didn't want to hear her answer.

"A dog."

He shook his head, anger creasing his eyes. "Dogs are a lot of trouble, Crissy. You have..."

"I'll take care of him, Daddy!" She stomped her foot impatiently. "I will, I promise. I'll buy the food and walk him and take him to the vet and everything. I know all about it."

"No, you don't. You've never had a dog."

"Well, maybe I did and you just didn't know about it."

He stared at her, suddenly alert and appearing alarmed. "Crissy, we cannot have a dog around here. Not right now. Is that understood?"

Crista stalked over to her pile and scraped at the leaves furiously. A moment later she threw down the rake and ran into the house. As she closed the door, she turned and looked out. Her father was watching her with a look of despair darkening his face.

Before he could say any more she bolted to her bedroom. Once she had slammed the door shut behind her, she hurled all the pillows and stuffed animals against the wall, then fell down by her bed and cried.

Monday afternoon, Crista hurried up to Nadine's still angry, still hurt. "He doesn't listen to me at all. He'll hardly even discuss it," she raved, throwing her arms up in the air and pacing in Nadine's living room. Nadine sipped some tea. Her full belly kept her from hunching over the table.

"Some fathers are like that, Crista," Nadine chided. "And your dad has some things still hanging out to dry."

Crista stopped and gazed at Nadine. "I know that. But he can't just dry up and die himself."

Nadine's voice was kind and low. "He really loved your mother a lot, didn't he?"

Stopping, Crista sighed. "Yes. Mama loved him, too. She was always telling me how they met in college and how they went to Bermuda on their honeymoon and how glad they were when I was born and all that stuff. She talked all the time. Sometimes it made him mad. But..."

"He's probably not a talker, either."

Crista sighed and sat down, putting her head on her hands. "What am I going to do, Nay?" She had been calling Nadine "Nay" for some time now, like Johnny did. Nadine called her Crissie when she was in a kissy-huggy mood.

"Well, the dogs slept the night in the yard, if that's any comfort."

Instantly brightening, Crista said, "They did?"

"They're gone now. I guess you noticed. But they go into the woods each day, most of the day. Then they come back at dinnertime. After they get your scraps they come here for mine." Nadine laughed, a musical titter.

Just as abruptly Crista hunched back over the table, her chin on her knuckles. "Lot of good it'll do. I'll never have a real pet."

Nadine patted her hand. "Believe me, your dad is all right. He's just working through some things. You want to hear bad, let me tell you."

"What?" Crista answered, looking up with interest.

Nadine grimaced. "Johnny's dad was an alcoholic. He couldn't keep a job. Johnny's mom holds it all together, even now. She's wonderful. Everybody wants her to divorce Johnny's father, but she won't hear it. And my mom and dad, well . . ." Nadine's voice cracked slightly, but she continued, "We were in an auto accident and they were taken to the emergency room. The doctor on duty supposedly had some personal problems and he completely blew it. They said he was drunk, but I guess the hospital covered it up. I was only six years old, no relatives. So my mom and dad died. Believe me, I know what it feels like to lose your family like you lost your mom, Crissie." Nadine's eyes glimmered with tears and she looked away. "But you just have to work through it," she rasped, catching her breath. "It takes time, but you get through it—with the Lord's help and some loving people around you. Like the people at the home."

"What home were you in?" Crista said, trying to ease Nadine out of her sudden mood.

"It was called Bethany Place. A church-run orphanage. I was lucky. I could have ended up in foster care all my life." She shrugged. "So count your blessings, Crissie."

Crista hung her head a moment. "I know. My dad's a good guy. It's just that there's so much I'd like to do and say. I just wish we could talk about Mama like she existed once. I think, All right, she died—we can't change that. But we don't have to act like she never was, like we never loved her or knew her."

Suddenly her eyes filled with tears and she put her head down. "It's never been the same, Nay. Never been. It's like the center of our lives was just cut out. And I know he blames me."

Nadine touched Crista's head and twined her hair in her fingers. Crista remembered how her mother used to do that, and for a moment it only made her feel worse. But as Nadine's soft hands smoothed and caressed her head and her cheek, she closed her eyes and felt calmer. A few minutes later she raised her head and wiped her eyes.

"I'm sorry."

Nadine shook her head. Her green eyes were sober, calm, kind. "Believe me, I understand, Crissie. Somehow it'll work out, though. I'm sure of that."

Sighing and letting the emotion drift away, she turned to look out the doorway. Rontu and Tigger stood out in the yard, panting, their tongues hanging out like a shirt arm flapping on a clothesline. She laughed, jumped up, and ran out. Tigger scurried back, but Rontu let her hug him. He stood there regally stiff, his long sandpapery tongue running up Crista's cheek. Nadine stood in the doorway and laughed. "Come for your handouts, I expect."

·13·
Wounded!

Rontu and Tigger not only visited both the Semms' property but also began standing at the edge of the highway waiting for Crista after school. In early November, Tigger for the first time let Crista pet him. Close up, his gouged eye looked terrible. But it was obviously an old wound and had healed as best as it could in the wild. Crista took several trips to the dump to collect things for her artwork. Rontu and Tigger followed like two vigilant soldiers, keeping the other dump dogs at a safe distance.

On two occasions Johnny shot rats with a .22 rifle he had, and Crista watched. She didn't much like the shooting of even rats, but she thought it was better than killing other animals. Johnny, however, was looking forward to the upcoming deer hunting season before Thanksgiving. Crista dreaded seeing some deer carcass hanging from a tree or the edge of the porch. But she knew she had no right to try and stop him. They needed the meat. Johnny wasn't making a lot of money at the service station.

Then on the second week of November Crista crossed the highway into the woods. Neither Tigger nor Rontu waited on the trail. Instantly Crista was worried. She hurried up the leafblown trail, listening intently for their barks of greeting. Squirrels and chipmunks frolicked about, but otherwise the woods were silent. Evening came early.

As she came around the bend at Elbow Rock, Tigger suddenly bolted out of the woods barking madly. His whole body shook, but his tail was wagging. Crista knelt down to pet him. There was blood on his nose, but no wound. "Where's Rontu, boy?"

He turned and dashed up the path, barking angrily. Crista came over the rise to The Love Tree and saw him. Rontu lay on the ground, his left flank a mass of blood. Her heart suddenly banging wildly inside her chest, Crista ran up the rest of the hill and stooped beside the big dog. He raised his head, then lay it back down, whimpering.

"You were shot!" Crista cried the moment she looked at the wound. It was a sure bullet hole. She saw the gouge in his white flesh where it went in just below the thick part of his rear flank. She gingerly lifted his leg. On the other side a mass had torn out. Crista peered up the trail and off into the woods. Patches of blood dotted the ground. He had dragged himself here.

She knew that hunters roamed the woods looking for deer and possibly bear. But no one could mistake a white Great Dane for a brown-haired deer. *Unless the hunter was just using him as a sick excuse for a little fun*, Crista thought bitterly. Her heart was hammering. "Please, Lord," she prayed, "let him be all right."

She took Rontu's head in her hands, kissing him. "Can you walk, boy?" She coaxed him with her hands, but he couldn't rise. He panted softly. His eyes looked glazed.

Crista opened her pack. She had nothing that she could use to drag him except her parka. But it was barely above freezing in the woods. No snow yet, but cold. She knew she had to go for Johnny and Nadine. But Nadine was big with the baby and probably couldn't help. Johnny would be working. Home was closer. And downhill.

But could she take him home, put him in the basement? What would her father say? What would she do with Tigger? She was sure he wouldn't leave Rontu's side.

As she inspected the wound again, she noticed her mouth was dry and her heart had slowed to a steady pound. Her temples rang with the beating. Her nails dug into her palms. Was she that afraid?

Think! she told herself. *He can't stay out here tonight. He'll die for sure.* But what would her father say? She knew she couldn't drag Rontu all the way to Nadine's. Besides, they had no real medical supplies. At least at home there was ointment and gauze, tape and iodine. She could bandage him. The basement was huge. Probably if Rontu was quiet, her father wouldn't even know he was there.

She knew she had to chance it.

Jerking off her jacket, she lay it gently under Rontu's head. The frigid air bit through her sweater and blouse. She pulled her ski hat down tight and tugged her mittens back on. "I'm going to get a blanket," she said. "I'm taking you home."

Rontu's ears bent back and his eyes flickered open. But he closed them after a few blinks. *He's going into shock*. She knew that from some first aid courses she had taken.

She knelt down next to Tigger. "You have to protect him now, boy. He's your friend and you can't let any of the dump dogs come around. They might try to hurt him. You understand?"

Tigger whined and licked her hand.

"I'm just going home for a few minutes. Then I'll be back. Okay? You just hold tight, okay?"

Rontu's ears wiggled, but he didn't open his eyes. His leg jerked, then stopped. Tigger eyed him worriedly, then turned back to Crista, his one deep brown eye quiet and trusting.

"Okay. Just wait. I'll be right back."

The cold wind blew through her sweater and made her shiver. But she jumped up and sped down the hill. She crossed the highway almost without looking, unlocked the cellar door and opened it, then ran up the basement stairs into the house. Her boots clattered on the floor as she gathered the gauze and other first aid supplies from the cabinet by the bathroom. She put it all into her backpack. Then she returned downstairs and grabbed the brown Navy beach blanket they used in the summer. It was ratty, but strong enough to drag Rontu in. She took down her father's hunting jacket off the hook by the stairs and put it on. It was big and warm. She rolled up the sleeves so her hands stuck out easily. She hurried out. Already the sun was setting.

In the doorway she paused, thinking she needed something else. The flashlight! She ran to the cellar walkway and picked up the big Eveready her father kept there. She flicked it on. No light. She gritted her teeth, remembering how she had last used it and it had been going out.

Then she spotted eight fresh D-size batteries on the shelf. She opened the flashlight, dumped out the eight bad batteries, and put the new ones in. The light switched on immediately. On a sudden impulse, she also grabbed the hunting knife and the Boy Scout hatchet lying against the wall.

Then she ran out the front door, forgetting to lock it.

Tigger's golden eye greeted her in the light of the flashlight as she came up the trail to where Rontu lay. Wagging his tail and whimpering, Tigger turned right around and hustled back up to his friend. As she knelt down by Rontu she patted Tigger's head. "Good boy, you stayed with him."

Rontu didn't move. Crista's heart seemed to stop. But she laid her ear on his chest. A fairly strong boomp boomp resounded. He was still alive. She shook his head. His eyelids flickered, but his breathing was shallow. Was she too late? She prayed as she took out the supplies. With the flashlight she examined the wound closely. Probably the best thing to do now was put on the iodized ointment to kill germs and wrap it.

She worked quickly. Rontu didn't respond to the sting of the ointment. She painted both sides of his leg with it, then soaked the gauze and applied a heavy layer to each side, wrapping it in a bandage and finally covering it all with paper tape. She tested it to make sure it wouldn't slip.

Around her the woods came alive with shrill noises—birds, chipmunks, the bark of a dog. Tigger sat patiently by watching everything with his one eye, his head cocked to the right. When Crista turned to him, he whined and licked her hand but didn't do anything else, as if he knew his job was protection, not nursing.

A frigid wind resounded in the tops of the trees. Her watch read past five. She had to get him into the basement and settled before her father came home.

She doubled the blanket over, then had second thoughts. She had seen Indians make drag beds on poles tied to the back of a horse. She knew how to fold the blanket over two poles to make a stretcher. That might be even faster than dragging him. Plus it would give Rontu a more comfortable ride.

Grabbing the flashlight, she pointed it to either side of the woods. Plenty of skinny trees were down all over the place. She had to find two that weren't rotten. After a few minutes of looking and testing, she found two poles she could use. With a little cutting using the hatchet, she stripped all the dead branches off and cut the narrow end down to size. She laid them over the blanket pointing downhill, then folded it around them, overlapping on top.

"Now for the hard part," she murmured as she gripped the still Rontu under the tops of his front legs and behind his head. He was heavy. Still, she pulled him down over the blanket, getting the main part of his body centered. His long legs hung out over the edge, but she knew that would be no problem.

After getting him onto the blanket, she took the rope, strung it around his shoulders, and lashed him into the stretcher so he wouldn't slip off. Finally, she hoisted the two long ends of the poles and held them under her armpits. The leverage was good. He wasn't as heavy as she had thought; he was still skinny.

She let down the poles, put on the backpack, gathered up everything she could find, then held the flashlight in her right hand as she lifted the poles once again.

She trudged ahead, dragging the stretcher with a grating noise on the rocky ground. In a minute she was panting and her shoulders hurt. Strangely, she thought of the story of *The Little Engine that Could* and began saying in her mind, "I think I can, I think I can."

Her forehead sweat into the ski hat. She finally pulled off the mittens and stuffed them into the hunting jacket side pockets, she was so hot. Tigger stayed right by her side, making a light padding noise with his feet. She noticed he was no longer limping. She had almost forgotten about his rescue from the trap.

She stumbled down the hill. Rontu's weight pounded in her armpits. Her forearms felt like gnarled pieces of wire. Her mind screamed, "You'll never do it." But she mumbled, "I think I can. I think I can."

Soon she saw lights whooshing by through the trees. "Only a little farther," she cried, now sure she would make it.

Her legs were tense with exhaustion. Then she hit a rock with the toe of her boot and fell. Everything clattered to the dirt. The flashlight hit the ground and went out. Tigger barked.

Crista sprawled, just wanting to lie there and forget she existed, but she forced herself back to her feet. She groped for the flashlight, found it, and shook it. The light didn't come on. Then she hit the button. Presto. She laughed, then swallowed back the dryness in her throat and heaved the poles to her elbows again. She plunged forward. Her legs felt like jelly.

Another car swished by. Only a few more yards to the road. She looked at her watch. Past 5:30. Just a little time left.

She reached the road.

Cars whizzed by, their headlamps like spears in the darkness. Tigger held back, but Crista waited on the shoulder, looking both ways for an easy cross. It was quitting time at work for many people, and traffic, though not heavy, was steady. Then no headlamp appeared in either direction.

Crista hauled the stretcher onto the pavement. Immediately the drag was worse than ever. Her feet slipped. Three lanes to cross.

Headlamps appeared in the darkness to her right. She had crossed one lane and was in the middle of the second. She had to go all the way.

The lamps swung into the straightaway. She turned her flashlight and shone it in the direction of the lamps so at least they would know she was there. Then she worried that Rontu might be slipping off. But he was tight. She took another deep breath and dragged with all her might.

She passed the second lane. The car didn't appear to be slowing. She waved the flashlight again. But it was only one more lane. She threw her back into it, bending down to push across.

A moment later she was all the way over. The car slowed, then ripped by with a honk on the horn.

"Thanks a lot, mister," Crista yelled, panting on the other side. Where was Tigger?

She shone the flashlight across the way. He stood on the edge of the woods, pacing and whimpering. "Come on, boy. You can do it. Just a little run for you. Come on."

She knelt down by Rontu and petted his head. He stirred slightly. His tongue flipped out of his mouth and lay on the blanket.

"Tigger, it's now or never. Come on." She waved at him. Tigger scurried back and forth in a panic. But he was getting closer to the road.

Crista stood, shining the flashlight right in his eye. "I'll show the way. Just follow the light." She rested the beam in the road so Tigger could see it. He stood on the edge of the road, pawing it.

"Come on, dumdum!"

Lights appeared on the road, this time on the other side.

"Hurry!" Crista stomped her foot. "Go!"

Tigger shot across. He reached the other side, wiggling and nuzzling her hand as if he had just won a prize. Crista gave him a hug, then hoisted the poles for the journey to the cellar. At least the road was slicked with oil to keep down the dust. It wasn't real slippery— just enough to make the dragging quicker. It was also flat. Not many humps and dips to worry about.

Panting heavily, she reached the last slope by the side of her house down to the cellar. Her father's car had not appeared. It was almost six o'clock. He would be home in less than a half-hour.

She pulled the stretcher down to the back doors, still open. A moment later they were inside. She jerked the string for the overhead light and all the dark things in the cellar suddenly became clear. Tigger followed her inside, hunched and looking warily from side to side.

"It's all right," Crista whispered. "No one's here."

Tigger slowly dropped down next to Rontu. The big dog stirred and whimpered, but didn't open his eyes.

"Thank You, Lord," Crista said. "He's still alive." She went into the downstairs bathroom to get towels, some blankets, and a mat for the bed. The three boats—the skiing boat, the sailboat, and the little punt—sat on trailers and sawhorses across the back where her father had laid them in the fall.

She began setting out a bed between the motorboat and the rowboat. The floor was concrete and cold, but with a layer of blankets it would be all right. The downstairs was much warmer than the outside.

Taking off the hunter's jacket, she hung it on the hook at the bottom of the stairs. Her shirt was damp. She listened for any signs of her father with heart pounding. Nothing.

She dragged Rontu over to the bed, pulled him off the stretcher, and laid him down on the rectangular area she had created. Tigger stood panting and watching.

"You can lie down next to him. Just be quiet." She put her finger to her lips.

Crista took the poles outside and laid them on the patio under the porch. She then ran upstairs and found two pots, one for water and the other for some food. She opened a can of beef soup, added water, and turned on the stove.

"Please don't come home, Daddy. Not yet."

She peered again into the medicine cabinet, but saw nothing she knew to use. The dressing she had done already would have to last the night. But if she told her father, he would know better what to do. He was a doctor. Certainly dogs were not that different from people.

But should she tell him? What if he made the dogs go outside?

Crista shivered and stirred the soup. The aroma of beef and vegetables drifted into her nostrils. It felt good to get out of the cold. The surface began to bubble a little. That was enough. She didn't want it too hot.

She poured the soup into the second pot and went back down the steep stairs. Tigger sat up, watching. Rontu lay quiet. She put down the water and the soup by Rontu's head. He stirred again and opened his eyes, then closed them without so much as a sniff.

"Go ahead," Crista said, patting Tigger's head. "You can have some. Just don't eat it all."

Tigger didn't move.

"Oh, you're going to be mannerly. Good." She rubbed his head and ears. He leaned into her hand with a yawn. How could dogs just accept things? she wondered with a smile, her heart filling with joy that now at last she had the two dogs in her home, if not quite welcome.

Crista ran back upstairs to get a big wooden stirring spoon. She would have to get something into Rontu. She knew that would get his body fluids running again, and it might help stop any infection. Didn't her mother always give her soup when she was sick?

She found the spoon and hurried back downstairs. Tigger hadn't moved or touched the soup or water. He sat in the dark shadow of the big motorboat on the trailer. He didn't seem afraid anymore. Maybe all he needed was that one big push to get him to come back to civilization.

In the cellar, the air was warm and the heater hummed noisily. Crista knelt down next to Rontu and cradled his head in her lap. She caressed his ears and dipped the spoon into the soup, just wetting it. "Come on, boy. Just a lick. Just lick the spoon."

His ears wiggled, but he didn't open his eyes. She painted soup onto his tongue, still draping out like a windless flag. It curled as she touched it, then shivered. She waited, dipped the spoon again, and spread it onto his tongue. This time there was the first movement of a lick.

"Good boy. Now a full lick."

The long pink tongue scraped up the front of the spoon slowly. Then a blue eye popped open. He blinked several times, then closed them. But this time he licked. Crista dipped the spoon again. It was getting all over her pants, but she couldn't worry about that.

She looked at Tigger and pointed to the soup and water. "Go ahead. You don't have to wait till he's done. This isn't master and slave here."

Tigger wagged his tail, stood, and eased over to the soup. He gave a quick lick, then looked up. Crista smiled. "Go ahead. It's all right. It's for you."

Soon the smaller dog ate with great gulps.

"Not too much now," she said, dipping the spoon again.

Rontu licked slowly and weakly. He was alive. Twice Crista bent down to listen to his heartbeat. It was stronger than before. She silently thanked God, and went on feeding him.

Tigger finished most of the bowl of the soup, but Crista was sure Rontu had gotten enough for now. She would feed him again later that night. How she would do that without her father knowing she wasn't sure. She still debated whether to tell him. Surely he wouldn't send the dog out into the cold!

She gave Rontu a little water. Tigger lay down on the edge of the blanket, curling up, his wiry brown-matted tail pulled around him. Crista petted him and Rontu together. "You guys'll be all right. Believe me, I won't let Daddy throw you out. But it would be better for you to be quiet."

She prayed that God would not let them bark.

Then, with back bristling, Tigger jumped up growling. Crista listened and heard the door open at the front door. Her father's muffled voice called out. Tigger barked.

Immediatedly Crista grabbed his muzzle. "Be quiet. You have to be quiet."

Tigger looked at her with his good eye, then stood motionless.

"Crista! Are you home?"

Crista unwrapped herself from Rontu, gave Tigger a pat, and whispered, "Just be quiet and everything will be okay." Tigger sat back, looking at her questioningly but not barking.

She hurried toward the stairs. "I'm down here, Daddy." She gave the dogs one last look, put her finger to her lips, and bounded upstairs. Shutting the door quietly behind her, she said, "I was just down in the basement."

Her father took off his coat, hanging it on the hatstand by the door.

"Dinner ready?"

"Not yet."

He clumped down onto the sofa in front of the big stone fireplace. "Would you like to go to Eddie's tonight for some hamburgers?" It was a local restaurant they sometimes visited.

"No!" As Crista said it, she realized she was a little too abrupt. She wiped her hands on her jeans, trying to cover the soupy spot. "I mean, I'll get dinner ready very quickly."

He chuckled and picked up the paper. She walked off into the kitchen and thought quickly about what to make. Grilled cheese and soup. That was easy.

She heard her father make a fire in the fireplace. Crista bent over the stove as she poured in the minestrone soup. Her father liked the chunky kind and lots of it, so she made two big cans. She buttered the bread and sandwiched the American cheese between the slices. But she knew she should go down and assure Tigger it was all right. She called to her father, "Just going down to the basement for something."

He didn't answer.

She opened the door quietly. The moment she did, Tigger made a raspy woof. Not loud. She closed the door behind her and hurried down the stairs. When she reached the bottom, Tigger bounded over to her, licking her hand. "It's okay, Tig. Is Rontu all right? You have to be quiet now. You have to be real quiet."

She bent down over Rontu. His eye opened and his tongue swished out. Then he closed his eye again and was still. She listened to his heartbeat. Strong. Steady. "It'll be all right," she whispered. She gave Tigger another friendly pet, then whispered to him to lie down. He obeyed and watched her hurry back to the stairs. She turned to face them again. She rasped, "I won't be back for awhile. So you'll have to just rest easy. Okay? You've got to be dead silent. Okay?" She prayed furiously that God would keep them quiet, not sure whether that was the kind of prayer God would answer.

Tigger licked his chin. Rontu lay still, his breath coming heavily through his mouth. She looked around one more time, then clopped back up the stairs.

·14·

Disaster!

They ate in silence at the main table in the living room. The fire crackled behind her and Crista strained to hear any noises from the basement. The only sound was her father's spoon tinking in the ceramic bowl.

Finishing, he stood. He picked up his plates and headed out for the kitchen. Crista was right behind him, her sandwich only half-eaten. He laid the bowl and plate in the sink along with the glass. Then turning, he nearly bumped into Crista. He gave her a funny raise of the eyebrows, then sidled around her. He walked into the hall and paused at the doorway to the cellar.

For a moment, Crista stopped breathing as she listened.

But then he seemed to change his mind and continued on into the living room. Crista breathed out nervously. She hurriedly cleaned the dishes and set them on the rack to dry. Then she walked as casually as she could into the living room and sat down on the couch in front of the fireplace. He lay back in the easy chair reading another journal. For once she was glad he had so many. She sat on the couch between him and the cellar, hoping that if for some reason he got up, she would be ready.

For an hour he read. The clock on the mantel ticked. No sounds erupted from the cellar. When she thought it was all right, she went downstairs, gave the dogs a look and a pet, and made some noises at the workbench that pricked up Tigger's ears. Then she came back up. Her father looked up and smiled hesitantly, then turned back to the journal.

She sat down again on the couch and pretended to read a book she had gotten at the school library. Though she turned pages, she read nothing, watching her father over the edge of the book.

After another half-hour he rose and walked toward the kitchen. Crista waited, barely daring to breathe again, her heart in her mouth. He opened the cellar door.

Crista jumped up. "What do you want, Daddy? I'll get it."

"Just a screwdriver to fix that door handle."

"I'll get it!"

The door creaked all the way open. Crista grabbed the handle and opened it all the way, edging in between him. "I'll get it."

He squinted at her curiously, wrinkling his nose and lips. "The red-handled one," he finally said. "Phillips head."

She thought she knew what that was. But she would have to risk it. She knew the straight kind was called a flat head. *Just look for the red handle*, she told herself. She padded down the stairs. Tigger stood, baring his teeth. When he saw Crista, he stopped and sat down.

Motioning with her hand, she placed her finger to her lips, then scrambled to the workbench, looking frantically for the red-handled screwdriver. There were four of them on the rack in the little metal holders. She pulled one out and studied at it. It had a funny tip, like a star with grooves in it. Was that it? She pulled out the others and examined them. Two had the star pattern, two the flat. The star pattern must be the Phillips head, she thought. She tried to choose between the smaller and the larger, and then, taking no chances, she took both. She bounded up the stairs breathless. Her father was down the hall at the guest bedroom turning the doorhandle.

She handed him the screwdrivers, smiling. "There."

He sucked on his pipe and began working on the door, tightening the handle. She watched. After a moment he turned to her. "You can go now."

"I like to watch." She knew he would soon be done and taking the screwdrivers back. She had to prevent that.

He snorted and returned to his work. When he was done she held out her hand. "I'll take them back."

He shrugged and handed them to her. "You're certainly servantly tonight."

She smiled brightly. "Just doing my job." She scurried to the stairs and went down again. She made some noises at the workbench, visited the dogs, spoke quietly, petted them. Rontu's breathing was steady.

Then Tigger jumped up. She heard footsteps on the stairs.

"Daddy, what is it?" she yelled.

She reached to pull the light string over the dogs. Tigger barked and growled. Her father's face leaned down over the banister. "What's going on here?"

She knew he saw the whole thing in a moment.

"Please don't make me put them out, Daddy. One of them is hurt. Please, Daddy, please."

·15·

Dad's Answer

Her father stood on the stairs, blinking. He shielded his eyes from the light, then took out his pipe. Tigger barked again. Crista grabbed the scruff around his neck and held him back. She was afraid he might charge her father.

As her dad gingerly stepped down onto the mat at the bottom of the stairs, Tigger suddenly lurched forward, but Crista yelled, "Tigger, it's all right!" He didn't move any further. She held him by the loose skin, refusing to let go.

She glanced at Rontu. "He was shot, Daddy. A hunter shot him. I couldn't leave him in the woods."

Her father turned the corner and stood before them, still blinking in the light. "They're dogs from the dump."

"But they're good dogs, Daddy. I've taught them tricks. Every day I went out and fed them something. They're not vicious."

Her father stared at Tigger. "Good grief, the beast only has one eye."

Crista felt Tigger's muscles flex. He was still ready to attack. Rontu hadn't moved, hadn't even twitched.

With a raspy sigh the tall man surveyed the scene quietly. Crista waited. She could see his jaw was tight and he looked angry. "When did you bring them here?"

"This afternoon."

"You found him in the woods."

"I bandaged him up and dragged him down. I would have taken him somewhere else, but this was the closest." She noticed her heart pounding in her chest. Tigger relaxed under her grip. Her father didn't come closer.

"They'll have to be put out," he said.

Crista wailed, "Daddy, he'll die."

"They're full of ticks and fleas and diseases. This is no place to nurse a dying dog. Good heavens, Crissie, think. You should have asked me before you brought them here."

"Daddy, there wasn't time." She knew she was losing control. He couldn't make her put Rontu out. Maybe Tigger could sleep outside the back door, but Rontu was sick.

"He can barely eat, Daddy. And there's a big hole in his hind leg. He was shot by a hunter. And he's sick. Daddy, you can't make him go out."

In the light, her father looked like a giant. He sighed heavily. He turned to go up the stairs.

Crista let go of Tigger. He didn't move. She ran to the stairs and grabbed her father's pant leg. "Please, Daddy." She was crying now. "I'll clean up everything. They won't bark, I promise. I won't let them make any messes. Just two weeks until he's well. Just two weeks."

She could see him looking at Rontu through the stairs. It was a better angle, a better view.

"What does he have on his hip?"

Hope surging into her heart, she turned to look. "I bandaged him up."

Her father shook his head with frustration. "I'm going upstairs, Crista. I'll look at the wound. Then when he can walk again, out they go."

Crista closed her eyes and said "Thank you," under her breath. A minute later he returned with a bunch of medical supplies, his doctor's bag, gauzes, and ointments. Tigger didn't rear up when he descended the stairs, but Crista held him as her father bent over Rontu.

"I'm going to give him a shot. First, an antibiotic. I hope it'll be okay. I'm not a veterinarian, Crista, but there isn't one for 20 miles. And it's past hours. If he's going to die from the wound, he would have by now. If there's any infection, this should stop it. Then I'll anesthetize the leg so I can sew him up."

Rontu didn't even flinch as her father gave him a shot of a clear liquid. Crista didn't ask what it was. After a few minutes, Dr. Mayfield gave him another shot, then removed the dressing and cleaned the wound. "What did you put on it?" He didn't look up.

She pointed to the tube of reddish iodized ointment in the array on the blanket. He nodded. "Well, at least that was smart."

He took out scissors, some stringy stuff, and a needle. Crista chewed her lip. Tigger stood back watching. No one seemed to breathe except Rontu, who hadn't moved. Her father opened an eyelid, shining a light in it. The sheer blue looked like a jewel in the light. He listened to the big dog's heart with a stethoscope, then waited. He pinched the dog hard on the leg. It didn't flinch.

Satisfied that the leg was sedated, he positioned the flashlight on the edge of the boat trailer so that the light shone directly on the gory-looking hole. After applying more ointment and some other items that Crista didn't recognize, he began sewing up the wound with the needle and catgut. When he did the inside of the leg, he had Crista hold it up. He didn't say anything as he worked. She noticed beads of sweat on his forehead as he worked. He dressed the wound the same way Crista had done. She watched with satisfaction that she had done it right.

Finally the job was finished. He gathered up his things.

"In bed at ten o'clock," he said. "The little one goes out in the morning. No days off from school. He'll be able to walk in a week or so. I won't take dog food out of your allowance, but they both go back to the woods when the big one is well. No arguments."

He headed up the stairs. They creaked. Then he sighed and walked back down.

"Crista," he said as he bent over the banister.

"Yes?"

He coughed. "You did the right thing. I'm proud of you. That took a lot of courage. But please understand, I'm just not ready for more responsibility right now."

He peered at her plaintively, then she ran to him and hugged him hard. He didn't seem to know what to do with his hands, but then as he held her she wept. A minute later they untangled themselves and he went upstairs. She called, "Thank you, Daddy. I love you."

"I love you too, Honey."

Crista sat by Rontu and petted him a long time. Tigger nuzzled her fingers and licked them. Tears burned again into her eyes as she caressed Rontu's ears. "Thank You, God," she whispered. "Thank You. Thank You."

The dogs were quiet all night, and in the morning Rontu's eyes were open, though he wasn't sitting up. Tigger was eager to go out. They hadn't messed the floor, but Crista knew Rontu probably had to go. She prodded him, but he wouldn't move. Finally she laid down some newspapers. "Go on this if you can," she said. "But if you can't, don't worry about it."

She gave them Cheerios and milk for breakfast. She made sure the water bowl was full. She let Tigger out and told him to play in the backyard, but not to go far. She tried to explain why he couldn't stay inside. But he just cocked his head and then trotted off up the driveway to do his business.

At breakfast, Crista and her father ate in silence. He read the paper. She finally got ready to go. When she stood at the door, he still hadn't said anything. She turned and looked at her father, bent over the paper.

"Daddy?"

He looked up.

"Thank you. Thank you from the bottom of my heart."

He nodded. "It's the only thing to do," he said. As she went out the door, he said, "The little one went up the road toward the highway."

She stopped. "I call him Tigger."

He nodded. "Tigger went up toward the highway."

"The other one's name is Rontu."

A smile quivered onto his face, then he turned, with some redness flushing his cheeks, back to the paper. Her heart racing, she closed the door quietly behind her, then ran up to catch the bus. The two other kids from down the street were already there when she arrived. Her breath came in great huffs of white in the cold air. They said hi and the three of them talked, but her mind was on her father. Something was happening inside him. She knew it. She sensed it. Maybe this was the thing they needed. Maybe this would really release the plug on their feelings for one another.

Crista watched the woods for a sign of Tigger, but she didn't see him. When the bus came, she got on in time to see her father's car pull around the bend.

She sat down in the seat with her friend Betsy and looked out the window. As the bus pulled away, her father reached the highway. She waved, but he didn't wave back. She figured he didn't see her. She wondered again if he hurt as much as she did about the death of her mother and if he really did blame her. She prayed that soon they would talk about it. Then she looked back and saw his car following the bus. It passed on a straightaway and he was gone.

Betsy tugged at her sleeve. "What's with you this morning?"

Crista turned to look out the window again. "I'll never understand my father," she said.

Betsy nodded. "I know. Mine's kind of weird too."

·16·
Out!

By the second day Rontu stood up and walked to the door on three legs. Dr. Mayfield had called a local vet and confirmed he had taken the right steps. The third day he went outside. Tigger was back each evening when Crista returned from school. She nursed Rontu, changing his bandage each day. He didn't worry at it like most dogs, trying to pull it off. Her father came down each evening for a look. Rontu didn't growl and neither did Tigger. He petted them gently, looked at the wound, grunted that it looked like it was healing, and went back upstairs.

By the weekend Rontu gingerly set down the back leg and limped on it. Crista decided to visit Nadine on Saturday morning with Tigger to explain why she hadn't come by. Nadine was concerned and Johnny raved angrily about hunters taking potshots. Both assured Crista that Rontu had a home there as long as she wanted him to.

The week mark passed and her father still knelt down each night beside Rontu looking at the wound. A wet scab covered it, but it was healing. Crista could see the black stitches like the lacing on a baseball holding the one-inch hole together.

After feeling all over the haunch, Dr. Mayfield made Rontu stand. He lifted the leg, backed him up, walked him forward. Tigger watched from under the motorboat, his belly resting on the cool floor. The dank smell of the basement had been replaced by a doggy smell which Crista had never known before. She liked it better than the normal basement smell, but she also knew this might be the last night they would be together. After this, it was either the woods or Nadine and Johnny's.

"I think he'll be okay," Dr. Mayfield finally said. He rose and put his hands on his hips, then turned to go out.

"I guess I should take them out tomorrow."

"That was the agreement," her father said. "But you can give them another day or two, just to be sure." He placed his loafered foot on the first step. The pipe smoke drifted upward. Crista liked the scent. The dogs seemed to like it too.

"Thank you, Daddy."

"One thing, though," her father said as if in pain. "They're not going to be pets."

Crista peered at her hands. "I know."

"As long as that's understood."

"Okay."

Crista realized now that keeping them at Nadine's was the best she could hope for. Rontu licked her hand as she stood looking across the room at her father. He bent over and knocked his pipe against his heel.

"Thank you for letting them stay for as long as they have, Daddy," she said.

He began to mount the stairs. Crista drew a long breath. She felt happy inside, but there was so much they needed to say to each other. When would it happen?

• • •

Two mornings later, Crista led the two dogs up to the road. Frost covered the ground in white specks on the leaves and rocks. Here and there a puddle had frozen. Next week was Thanksgiving. In a way, Crista longed to invite Nadine and Johnny over for dinner. She knew Nadine found it hard cooking and taking care of the place now that she was so big. She complained about her legs swelling and her headaches. She knew they probably wouldn't have a turkey. And Johnny hadn't bagged a deer yet.

She puzzled over the question as she hurried Rontu and Tigger across the road. Rontu still limped, but he put more weight on the foot now. He would be up to normal in no time—if he bedded down at the Semms. If he didn't, where would he go that was safe? Crista worried about it, but she prayed that they would be at Nadine's that night.

On the other side of the road, she bent down at eye height with Rontu. She held his jowels in her hands. "I want you to be at Johnny and Nadine's tonight, understand? Both of you. You have to keep warm. You're not completely okay yet. Understand?"

There were flecks of egg still on Tigger's chin. She had given them a hearty breakfast of pancakes and eggs before she made the same for her father. She didn't tell him what she fed them, though.

"No messing around about this," she said with a stamp of her foot. "No more dump stuff—got it?"

Rontu whimpered and Tigger wagged his tail. They both looked like they were ready to trot off for a delectable meal of fresh garbage. Then the bus roared in the distance and the two kids from her neighborhood came up on the other side of the road watching them.

"Okay, I have to go. Now get up there."

Both dogs jumped up and hurried back from the road, then turned when they reached the trees to watch her cross. She clambered onto the bus and sat down across from Betsy so she could see the dogs one last time. Betsy said, "I didn't know you had two dogs."

Crista said, "I don't. Not really." She didn't turn.

The bus rolled forward and the dogs watched, their pink tongues wiggling as they both panted.

"They're kind of ugly," Betsy said, looking over Crista's shoulder. All the kids on the bus were staring.

"They're friends," Crista said flatly. "When you're friends you don't care what they look like."

Betsy gave her a funny look and went back to her seat. Crista remained where she was. No one asked her any more questions after that. She didn't concentrate on school that day for worry. Even art class didn't interest her much. When the bus let her off, she didn't even say goodbye to Betsy. She hurried into the woods and disappeared up the path before the bus even pulled away.

•   •   •

Nadine lay on the bed alone in the cabin, her belly like a round mound under the covers. A fire crackled in the fireplace. She had her elbow over her eyes when Crista knocked and walked in. Crista hadn't seen either of the dogs outside. It was already getting dark and a wind was blowing up. But Crista had remembered to bring her flashlight in her pack to school.

"Hi," Nadine said in more of a moan than a greeting.

Crista hurried over the bed. "Are you sore?"

"Like a beat-up rag doll." Nadine patted her belly. "Look at me. If I'd known it would be like this, I wouldn't have gotten married." She laughed.

Realizing she was joking, Crista smiled. "Do you think it's close?"

"January first. That's my due date, I think. If I'd gone to a doctor, I would have given him April first as the conception. So I figure nine months, January one." She sighed and moaned. "I'm never going to make it."

"Where's Johnny?"

"Working. He's taking the last three weeks around Christmas off. Without pay. But we've been saving. Do you like the crib?"

Crista looked across the room in surprise. A shiny oaken crib with a mattress and plastic runners on the top edges stood there.

"Johnny found it at the dump. He finds everything at the dump now. It's a regular general store." She laughed again.

The crib looked old, but clean. Crista walked over to touch it. "It's pretty. How come someone would throw this away?"

"You'd be amazed at what people throw away. You've been there, haven't you?"

"Yeah, but I never saw a whole baby crib."

Moaning, Nadine rasped, "Could you bring me a cup of cold water, Crissie? I'd appreciate it."

Over the last month Johnny had found an old well on the property because of a pump he discovered in the shed. It was now flowing water. But no one was sure what would happen when everything froze. Crista filled a cup and brought it over to Nadine. She drank lustily.

"That's the best water I've ever had. Mountain water. We ought to bottle it and sell it. We'd make a fortune."

Nadine lay back down on the big pillow. "So are the dogs okay?"

"I was hoping they'd be here."

She shook her head wryly. "They haven't been. At least if they have, I didn't see them. Of course I've been lying around here like an old fat sow the whole day." She turned on her side and leaned on an elbow. "So your father really let you keep them there, huh?"

Crista shook her head. "Yeah, he even stitched Rontu up. I was surprised. I just hope Rontu doesn't tear out the stitches in a fight or something."

"They'll be here tonight," Nadine said, "if they remember the way. Don't worry, Crista, they can take care of themselves."

Crista shook her head. "Well, I'd better get back out on the trail. I wanted to put something out for dinner before I went home for the night."

"You're going all the way home, then back up the trail?"

"I guess."

"Then take some of those corn fritters we made last night and put them out for the dogs. They're in the icebox over there."

Crista opened the ramshackle box. Johnny had gotten the electric generator going and found out the refrigerator worked when a little electricity was pumped through it. A pile of the corn-studded pancakes perched on the shelf.

"Their dish is on the porch. Put in a bunch. Johnny said I burned them."

Crista peered at them and noticed they did look a little black. She laughed.

Shrugging, Nadine chuckled. "That's how we always made them. How was I supposed to know? Sometimes Johnny thinks I'm supposed to be a remake of his mother."

"Does he ever miss his family?" Crista said as she scrunched the pancakes into the bowl. Then she recovered the plate and set it back in the refrigerator.

"Yeah. We'll visit them soon. After the baby. They write every now and then." Crista felt Nadine's eyes running up and down over her. Nadine had a way of looking at you that made you feel approved, not criticized. "He's kicking again," she said suddenly. "Want to feel him?"

Wiping off her hands, Crista shuffled over and laid her hands on Nadine's stomach. She picked up on the kicking motion. "He feels all knotted up in there," she said.

Grinning, Nadine remarked, "Yeah, feels like about six of them in there now. That would be a real circus, wouldn't it?"

Taking her hands away, Crista said, "You still haven't seen a doctor?"

"Nope."

Crista sighed. "Nay, you really should have the baby in a hospital."

Immediately Nadine shook her head. "Now don't go giving me a lecture about it. I've read all the books and I made Johnny read them all. He's petrified. But we don't have health insurance and we'd be financially strapped for years. I'm not going in as a charity case."

"But what if there are problems?"

Nadine's eyes didn't move. "We'll handle them."

Swallowing, Crista ran her fingers along the edge of the bed. "I guess it makes kind of an exciting story."

"That's what I think," Nadine said enthusiastically. "And I'm sure things'll work out. If worse comes to worst, Johnny'll just rush me down the mountain in his truck and I'll go to the hospital as a charity case. But it'll be okay."

Leaning now against the crib, Crista looked around the cabin again. Nadine had made it homey. The painting she had done at Halloween, and later finished, hung over the fireplace. Two of the uglier deerheads were gone. There were several wreaths of paper flowers on the walls, as well as some pictures of family. It was clean. Now that they had some electricity, they were much better off.

Crista said, "Well, I'd better find those two mutts before they starve."

Nadine laughed. "They'll be there."

They were. Crista found them nosing around The Love Tree. She gave them the corn fritters and played with them. Afterward they followed her down to the road. But when they began to cross it, she stopped them, telling them they had to go to Nadine's. She repeated the names several times. Finally they both shuffled back into the woods and sat down looking at her resentfully.

They would be good pets, she thought. But she couldn't risk making her father truly angry. Somehow, though, she was sure now she would find a way to keep them.

She sprinted across the road, waved the flashlight, then descended the road toward her house. She prayed the dogs would have the sense to spend the night at Nadine and Johnny's.

·17·

The Contest

The week before Thanksgiving, Crista entered three pieces of acrylic art in a contest at school. One was a picture of Rontu standing on Elbow Rock like Robin Hood watching over Nottingham Forest. The second was of Nadine in the cabin doorway, her belly big and protruding. She wore a blue jumper with a white blouse, something Crista imagined rather than saw.

The third portrait was of her father. It was the biggest. In it, he sat looking out the picture window of the house. She had painted it as she imagined it might have appeared to someone looking in. She had a hard time getting the window reflection right, but in the end she was satisfied it was her best. She also planned to give him the portrait for his birthday in December and the one of Nadine to her for Christmas. The paintings would hang for a few weeks in the small library downtown. Judges would award prizes the day before Thanksgiving. There were many categories. Crista entered each in a different one: Rontu for "Animals," her father for "Relatives," and Nadine for "Country Life."

When the paintings were finally hung, a week before Thanksgiving, it was all Crista could do to contain herself. She wanted to show Nadine and Johnny first, to see what they thought. Then, if she had the courage, she would show her father.

That Saturday afternoon she pulled on her heavy blue parka, her mittens, and the red-and-white ski cap she always wore, then heaved on the backpack with some food for the dogs as well as some charcoal and drawing paper. She trekked up to Nadine's with Rontu and Tigger close behind. Nadine and Johnny were there. She knew Saturday was his new day off.

Nadine was hanging some clothes on the line in the cold air. Crista saw Johnny's rear end poking out the front of the shed as she marched into the yard, waving. "Kind of cold for clothes drying."

Smiling, Nadine said, "It's the only way." She wore a thick parka and red mittens. Her cheeks were red with the cold. The jacket could barely zip over her belly. Crista didn't think she had ever seen a pregnant woman so large.

"I have a surprise for you."

Nadine looked up with a clothespin in her mouth. "Not a dog in a trap."

"Nothing life-or-death this time."

"Look who's here," Nadine called to Johnny.

Poking his head out, Johnny wore a heavy flannel hunting jacket with black gloves and his green Eagles hat. It was already smudged with grease from working at the service station. "Hi, Crista." He smiled and adjusted his hat, then bent back into the shed.

"So what's up?" Nadine asked, pinning Johnny's blue work shirt up on the line.

"I entered a contest." Crista shuffled her booted feet and dug her mittened hands into her coat pockets. She didn't want to act proud about it, but she felt good. And excited.

"Art?"

Crista nodded.

Nadine squealed with pleasure. "I hope you didn't do something of me."

"You'll never know till you see it," Crista answering, cocking her head mysteriously.

"Oh, we couldn't go down to your house. Your father..."

"No, it's at the library."

"The library! Well, Crista makes the big time. What will you win?"

"Twenty-five dollars for first. Fifteen for second. Ten for third. They're judging them in a few days. I'm hoping to win something so I can buy Christmas presents." Crista didn't mention for whom. But she could tell from Nadine's eyes that she was about to protest.

"Don't worry," Crista said. "I wouldn't get you anything that cost more than 50 cents."

Nadine giggled. "Okay. So I guess you want us to take a break from our hard labors to see this marvel."

"These."

"These?"

"I have three of them in it."

"Three!"

Crista nodded. "I never felt so good about my artwork until now. I might even win."

"Johnny!"

The big man poked his head out of the shed again. "What? I'm doing something."

"Nothing that can't be done later. Come on. Get that old heap of yours in gear." Nadine grabbed Crista and hugged her. "I'm so excited. And I'll be able to say I knew Crista Van Gogh when she was just 12."

Crista laughed. Johnny stalked up to them a bit miffed, but when Nadine explained he didn't protest. He started the truck while Nadine went into the cabin to get her purse and put on some lipstick. When she ambled out they talked about what to do with the dogs and Johhny said, "Let them stand in the back of the truck. I've done it before."

He dropped down the gate and whistled. Both dogs jumped into the back after some coaxing from everyone. Then they began the jostly ride around the mountain.

The library was quiet, musty, and warm, with sharp straight sheets of light cutting down from some windows in the ceiling. Paintings hung all over the walls. Crista was about to lead them right to hers, but Nadine put up her hand and whispered, "Let me guess which ones. Did you sign them?"

"We weren't allowed on the front. Not until the judging is over."

"Good."

Johnny whipped off his cap and zipped open his jacket. Nadine and Crista hung up their parkas and hats over a bench by the front door. Then they proceeded around the hall. The categories were posted above the paintings. There was one for "People," another for "Farm and Country," a third for "City." Nadine and Johnny gazed up at the drawn scenes. Nadine clucked and hemmed and said, "No, not that one . . . No, not there either."

They passed from the front main wall to the side wall by the sofas and easy chairs. Crista walked behind them with her hands in her back pockets, restraining a smile. Surely they wouldn't pick out hers that easily. But deep down she hoped they would. And that they would like it.

They came to "Animals." There were several dogs, a gorilla behind bars at the zoo, some sheep and goats, a cat and a kitten. Nothing incredibly good. Nadine looked over the whole wall, continuing her clucking. The portrait of Rontu hung in the upper left-hand corner.

"That one!" Nadine cried as her eyes fell on it. She turned and looked into Crista's face.

Crista couldn't contain it. "Yes. It's Rontu."

"As if we didn't know!" Nadine turned around and took Johnny's hand. "It's so beautiful. And just like him. On the rock. That rock in the woods. It's great, Crista, really great. It has to win first."

Crista's face felt hot as a stout woman in a gray dress shushed them from the front desk. Other faces had turned and scowled. But Nadine kept talking, though a little lower.

"You've got his eyes perfect, Crissie. How do you do it? Look at those eyes, Johnny. I wonder how she'd do mine. And his face. You must have spent so much time on his face."

Grinning beside her, Johnny murmured, "Okay, Honey, I think you're embarrassing Crista."

The library was quiet and only papers rustled here and there as people turned pages. But Nadine spun around and put her arm over Crista's shoulder, pulling her tight. Crista dropped her chin but felt happy. They had recognized it, but that was the obvious one. Now for the other two. Well, she would be happy if they only liked them. She stopped herself and just crossed her fingers behind her back.

Nadine continued gazing at the painting. She stepped closer, though it was up high and not easy to look at very close. "And the rock. All the different grays and streaks and stuff. It's incredible. Where did you learn to do that?"

She didn't wait for an answer. "Oh, and look, Johnny, he's like the king of the forest or something." She giggled. "I wish I could paint like that." She gripped Crista and squeezed her shoulder with enthusiasm.

"Okay, one down. There're two more, Johnny, and I think they'll be harder."

They walked by more painting-laden walls. Nadine jumped at several other paintings, admiring them, but as she looked more closely at each, she shook her head. "Not Crissie's style. No, not that one."

Nadine took Crista's hand and they edged around the room, taking it all in. There were several very good pieces that Crista knew would be tough to beat. But of the sixth-grade paintings she honestly felt hers were among the best.

They came to several dividers used to hang more paintings and drawings. It was the one entitled "Country Life." Crista drew in her breath and waited. The very first one they came to was the one of Nadine in the doorway of the cabin. Johnny passed over it, but Nadine stared at it saying nothing. There was a sudden calm in the room, as if everyone was waiting to see what she would say.

"Crissie, it's beautiful."

Nadine turned and hugged Crista so tightly she couldn't breathe. But when she let go, her eyes were glimmering with tears. "I never had anyone do anything so beautiful for me."

"It's going to be my Christmas present to you."

"You're not going to sell it?"

Crista shook her head. "Of course not."

Nadine turned and breathed out with a long sigh. "Johnny, what do you think?"

A lopsided smile beamed onto his face. "I'm just glad it's not a nude."

The two girls laughed and the librarian gave them another frustrated look. Nadine whispered, "This is probably the most noise she's had in here since July Fourth."

They moved on. When they came to the "Relatives" section, again Nadine was right in picking Crista's portrait of her father. She stepped up to it and gazed at it longer than any of the others.

"It's for his birthday," Crista said. "I hope he likes it."

"He'll love it," Nadine said convincingly.

Crista shifted her weight uneasily. "I don't know about that."

"Take it from me, he'll love it. He may not say he loves it, but deep down he'll be crying, just like I was. You have talent, Crissie. And love. It's from the heart. Your paintings are from the heart. That's why they're so moving."

Her heart bumping loudly in her chest, Crista settled down as they took one more round at all the paintings. Finally Nadine said, "I give you three firsts.

If they don't win firsts, it's pure jealousy. You have to win."

"You really think so?" Crista looked into Nadine's deep green eyes and wished for all the world she was right.

"Absolutely," Nadine said. "Don't you agree, Johnny?"

Scratching his head and throwing his long, dark mop off his forehead, he said, "I'm not very good at this kind of thing, but I'd say they're some of the best. They definitely do something to you."

Nadine gripped Crista's hand. "See. It's settled. You win!"

Crista laughed and Nadine patted her on the back. As they walked out of the building, both dogs began barking. Crista felt a trembling excitement gush through her. More than ever she wanted her father to like it. Just to say he liked it. That would be enough.

·18·
Judgment Day

"What is this all about, Crista?" Dr. Mayfield asked as he lazed back in the easy chair reading the newspaper.

"It's just a little trip," Crista answered, trying to keep her voice casual enough that she wouldn't be disappointed if he said no. She stuck her hands in the back pockets of her jeans and crossed her feet, balancing on the right heel and toe.

"Why does it have to be tonight?"

"Because tonight is special."

"What's special?" Dr. Mayfield took his pipe out and gazed at her. There was no irritation in his voice, just an honest questioning.

Crista didn't want to tell him it was the night of the awards. In a way she was almost afraid to go herself. She thought she ought to simply come out and say it, but she wanted him to be genuinely surprised.

"Daddy, I just want you to take me down to the school and come in. Just for awhile. They're having a special event and if we don't get there by 7:30, it'll be too late."

Dr. Mayfield appeared irritated for a moment, but finally he pushed himself out of the big green layback chair. "I have a lot of work to do, so this had better be important. Tomorrow is Thanksgiving."

"I know. But it is important. You'll see." She almost jumped with excitement that he was actually going. Crista dressed and waited for him at the door. Her father dawdled in front of the mirror, murmuring to himself, but finally he appeared in the doorway, the pipe still stuck in his teeth, his brown mustache thick and heavy above it.

They drove down the main road in silence. Moonlight Mountain stood behind them as they neared the school on the other side of the cove from their cabin. A snow flurry started, then stopped. Frequently in the mountains snow fluttered down before Thanksgiving. Rarely did anyone in that area not have a white Christmas. For Crista, tonight was the night of all nights. She hoped she would at least receive an honorable mention. Deep down, though, she wanted a first—in all three categories. She suspected that was impossible. She would settle for a first in anything. One first would make her walk on air. Three? It was incredible just to wonder about it!

As Dr. Mayfield drove Crista coached herself not to think about it. But all those glowing hopes kept shooting to the surface like skyrockets in her mind. What would her father think if she won something? Would he say anything? The words "Great job, Crista," or "I loved it" would give her something to live on for a century.

The wiper blades of their blue Jeep Cherokee clicked lightly on the rubber seam around the front windshield. The snow—more like pieces of ice— ticked on the glass. Crista slumped in her seat watching the white flecks rush by. She imagined herself in a spaceship traveling at the speed of light into a far galaxy. On the planet they headed to, huge dogs like Rontu ruled. And Crista Mayfield was their chief artist, sent to make portraits of each of the subjects s their hairy snouts would be remembered forever. She giggled at the thought.

They came around the 90-degree curve to the main highway, then descended rapidly toward the school. The lights of the Wallenpaupack Gift Shop, open even in winter, and several gas stations blinked. The paintings had all been moved from the town library to the elementary school for the presentation.

When Dr. Mayfield turned into the school parking lot, cars looked stuffed into every possible space. Dr. Mayfield braked the Jeep on the turn and stopped. "What's going on here tonight?"

Crista smiled and snuggled deep into her parka. "Something special. Let's just go in."

He drove in, found a space, and parked. She caught him smiling brightly a few times and she realized he might even be a little excited. Certainly he was curious!

As they walked up the sidewalk to the main entrance, people greeted Dr. Mayfield and classmates said hello to Crista. John Barnes, a boy who had also entered the contest, came up behind her and covered her eyes with his hands.

"Guess who?"

"John Barnes!" Crista said, recognizing the voice.

Dr. Mayfield stopped and looked at the two. John said, "So you gonna win tonight, Crista?"

Crista felt herself blush. "Try to."

"Not if I have anything to say about it." He rushed by her, giving her a little nudge. Crista liked him, but he could be kind of proud and cocky at times.

"Who is that?" asked Dr. Mayfield. "And what contest?"

"A boy in my class." She grabbed his hand. "Come on, I'll show you."

People—mothers, fathers, kids—milled around in the big auditorium, shuffling from exhibit to exhibit. Crista began explaining. "I entered some of my pictures in the art contest."

Her father sucked on his pipe. Several people walked by and said, "Evening, Dr. Mayfield." He nodded to them and smiled. Crista found herself thinking, *I wish he would smile at me like that.* But she pushed it out of her mind. *No*, she told herself, *I want more than that. But I'd settle for it.*

"So which ones are yours?"

"You have to guess."

Dr. Mayfield sighed unhappily, but to Crista he suddenly appeared more attentive than usual. An explosion of excitement resounded deep down in her breast. She said, "These are all animal pictures here."

Looking them over, her father asked, "Is one of yours here?"

"Guess."

He shook his head in wonder. "They're all very good." He drew on his pipe and blew out smoke rings.

Then an elderly lady, someone Crista didn't know, clattered up behind them. "Hey there, Dr. Mayfield. How's it feel to have a little Picasso in your family?" She winked at Crista.

Dr. Mayfield smiled at her. "Hello, Mrs. Campbell."

Suddenly Crista remembered one of the judges was named Campbell. She felt a sudden squeeze of terror in her throat.

Glancing at Crista uneasily, Dr. Mayfield said, "What brings you out tonight?"

"Oh, that grandson of mine. Draws everything under the sun. Thinks he's going to win a trip around the world." She tittered. "We grandmothers have to encourage them. He's certainly not as talented as some." She raised her eyebrows again in Crista's direction.

Crista barely dared to breathe. Had she really won something?

Dr. Mayfield seemed to forget about picking which painting he thought was Crista's and they moved on to the next panel. They passed most of them, including the one of Nadine, when the announcer asked everyone to be seated. Crista's heart began pounding as the judges gathered up front and the announcer went through a few points, made jokes, and introduced the panel. Mrs. Bevans, the art teacher, gave a quick speech and several others talked. Finally the announcer, a heavyset man with a booming voice, said, "Now we will grant the awards."

Crista shrank back in her seat, her hammering heart so loud she thought the whole room must hear. She kept blinking and swallowing and telling herself if she didn't win, it didn't matter. But it did. It meant everything to her.

The big man reeled off several categories ahead of Crista's. She knew most of the kids who won and clapped gladly. But her heart was still in her mouth.

Then they came to the animal portraits. Crista could barely think. Her ears seemed to pick up every noise. A whooshing noise filled her head.

"Third place," the announcer said. "John Barnes for his picture of Keefe, his aunt's cat."

Two places to go, Crista thought.

John bounced up and took his award with a bow as the painting was displayed and everyone clapped.

Crista's eyes roved the crowd and suddenly she saw Nadine and Johnny. Nadine had turned and was gazing at her brightly. She mouthed, "You're going to win!" then gave Crista a thumbs-up. Crista looked away, her face hot.

"Second place," the announcer said. "Carolyn Wisniewski for her painting of Lightning, a horse."

Her whole body frozen in place, Crista's mind screamed, *Have I really taken first?*

After Carolyn's applause died, the announcer said, "And first place..."

Crista almost rocketed out of the seat.

"Bill Plante."

She didn't even hear the rest. She was so stunned, she sat there afraid she would burst into tears. *Bill Plante? Bill Plante*! her mind echoed. *He got first? But what about...*

She didn't dare look at Nadine or Johnny. Her father calmly smoked and clapped. But her whole world had stopped. She hadn't taken a thing. She had put everything she had into that painting. Didn't they see it was Rontu? On the rock? Her friend?

But no one heard her thoughts and a sinking terror gripped her. What if she didn't win anything? Nothing?

They went through other categories, then came to the one on Country Life. Again Crista went through the same agony. "Third place, Lou... Second Place, Elizabeth... First Place..."

Her knees were pressed so tightly together that she almost screamed with the waiting. Surely she had...

"Barbara Reeves for..."

Crista's eyes filled with tears. They hadn't liked anything. She was horrible. She was a terrible artist. Everyone had lied. Even Nadine. The paintings stunk.

She wanted to run from the room. It was true—she was nothing. Not even her father was interested. He wouldn't have reason to say a thing. He would never think she did anything right.

It was all she could do to remain in her seat. She blinked back the tears and the choking sensation that squeezed her throat. She glanced in Nadine's direction, but even her friend stared ahead, fixed to the spot. Nadine probably realized how heartbroken she was and didn't want to hurt her any further by looking at her. Crista just wanted to dash out and never come back.

They came to the "Relatives" category. But Crista had lost all hope. It ended up as she thought: not a single award. This time John Barnes took a first and it stung the way he smartly received it, like he owned the world. Crista sank deep into her seat, hating herself, God, the world, and everyone else. She should have stayed at home. It had all been for nothing. Her lip quivered so hard it was all she could do to keep from sniffling.

Nadine's head stayed straight ahead.

Her father smoked his pipe. He hadn't even looked in her direction.

She had been a fool. To think anyone would think her a painter, let alone an artist. No wonder her father rarely said he loved her. She was a little nothing. There was no reason for him even to like her.

She slipped lower in the seat. Her chin quivered and any moment she was afraid she would break. But somehow she held the tide back.

Just get it over with, her mind yelled. *Just let me go home now!*

The announcer walked stoutly to the microphone for the last time. Crista stared at her booted feet. A tear dripped off the end of her nose and splatted on the brown leather. She barely heard what the announcer was saying.

"After all the judging . . . a special talent, a remarkable talent . . . a special award . . . something never done before . . . might have won several categories . . . For that reason we've presented the Cloris Blackmun Endowment Award to . . ."

There was a long pause. Crista closed her eyes.

Then the words "Crista Mayfield" boomed across the room.

Everything seemed to stop around her. She saw her father's leg tense, then she felt his eyes on her. She looked up.

"Get up there," her father said suddenly, a broad smile on his face.

Crista blinked. Everyone had turned to look in her direction. The announcer said, "Crista, please come up."

She stood, her legs suddenly going weak. She rubbed at her eyes. She saw Nadine looking at her with a huge smile and Johnny grinning next to her. People were already clapping.

"Go up. You won the whole show," her father said.

Crista was too stunned to speak. She stumbled over seats, by a fat woman, past a boy in her class, by two more adults, into the aisle.

The announcer said, "The judges have agreed that Crista's three paintings will be displayed in the library until Christmas, and we'd like to have one there permanently."

Crista staggered forward, her heart hammering through her ribs. She still wasn't sure what it was all about. But in less than a minute she knew. She had won a special grant of 200 dollars, private art lessons for six months with a local artist, and a trip to Philadelphia to the Art Museum there.

Everything after that was a blur. Kids congratulating her. Nadine shrieking with joy and hugging her with her belly big as a watermelon. Johnny patting her on the shoulder. Her art teacher, Mrs. Bevans, kissing her on the cheek. Even her father was surrounded with well-wishers. The three paintings were displayed at the front and people passed by them commenting and enthusing. Several smaller kids even asked for her autograph.

It was only when everyone was leaving that she got a moment with her father. He said, "So this was your surprise?"

"*My* surprise, I think," Crista said, still dizzy with the thrills of the evening. "I was never so surprised in my life."

For a brief moment he hugged her, but then he let go as if slightly embarrassed at the show of emotion. "I knew you loved painting. I just never realized how important it was to you. I'm sorry, Honey," he said, blinking and trying to regain his composure. For awhile he admired the paintings at the front. Even though he said little, she felt as if the whole world knew what had happened.

As they drove up the road, he was quiet; there was a comment about the weather, another remark about the surprise. The snow had stopped. It was just frigid air that greeted them when they stopped in the parking place at the front of the yard. Crista began to open the door to get out. She told herself just to remember that what mattered was that others told her how good it had all been.

But as the door cracked open and the light inside came on, her father's voice murmured quietly behind her, "Crista?"

She turned. His eyes paused to fix on her a moment, then looked down. He wasn't even smoking his pipe.

"Crista, why didn't you ever show me these things?"

She sucked her lip a moment. "I did, Daddy. Sometimes."

He nodded and sighed. "I guess I was immersed in a journal or something."

She looked at the glove compartment.

"I'm sorry. I wish I'd known. You have a talent like your mother."

"Mother?" Crista's eyes grew wide.

"She painted in college. High school, too. And before. She stopped after we got married."

"How come?"

He smiled. "She told me you were her art."

Crista's chest tightened.

"Crista, please understand..." His voice became husky. "I wish I could talk about..."

Suddenly she threw her arms around his neck. "It's okay, Daddy. I understand."

He pushed her back far enough so he could see her face. There was a glint of a tear in his eye. "You don't understand. I don't understand. It hasn't been easy. I'm..."

He looked away. Suddenly he hit the horn. "Why do I find it so hard?"

He turned back to her. Crista felt as though her heart would leap out of her chest.

He sighed heavily. "I'm proud of you, Honey. I've always been proud of you. But..."

She grabbed him around the neck and held on.

Suddenly he was crying. His whole chest heaved. "I'm so sorry. I'm so sorry. I'm so sorry."

They held each other for over a minute, Crista's arms about his thick neck and shoulders. The hug seemed to go on and on. It was a strange, warm, glowing feeling inside that she had never felt before. She sensed that he did not want it to end. But finally he let go and they got out of the Jeep.

They got ready for bed quietly in their rooms. But as Crista sat on her bed to pray, he suddenly appeared in the doorway. He said, "You made me glad to be alive tonight, Crista, glad to have you as my daughter. Thank you for your surprise. But more than that, I thank God for you."

She smiled, a golden glow deep in her heart. "Thank you for going."

"We have to do that kind of thing more often." He smiled and then said, "Would you like to pray together tonight?"

Together they knelt by the bed. They prayed for each other. They thanked God for the awards. And

Crista ended by saying, "Thank you for giving me to Daddy, Lord." They hugged again and she smelled the smoke on his breath. Then he tucked her in and went out, flipping the light switch as he went into the hall. She felt secure and happy, happier than she had felt in nearly a year.

·19·

The Truth

Crista wanted more than ever to tell her father about Nadine and Johnny, but she honestly felt she couldn't betray their trust. She also longed to talk to him about Rontu and Tigger. But the two dogs seemed happy staying in the shed at the Semms' place.

Then one night the week after Thanksgiving, as they sat in the living room with a crackling fire, Crista decided to be bold. She asked him, "Daddy, how come you don't deliver babies anymore?"

He looked up from a novel he was reading and sighed. "It's a long story, Honey."

He'd used that word several times lately. *Honey.* Crista rolled it over in her mind. Like what Johnny sometimes called Nadine. She liked it.

"Well, we have all evening," she said.

He put the book down. She had been asking him more questions lately. He hadn't seemed so quiet since the night of the awards. He sat up in the chair, pulling in the leg rest. "Something happened to me after your mother was killed."

She waited, barely daring to breathe.

"I was very upset. For those first months I could barely think, even in the operating room. Several people told me to take a vacation. I thought by immersing myself in my work, I would get over it. But..."

His voice got husky again, like he might cry. She waited, breathing shallowly.

"I didn't always think. When there were emergencies in the delivery room, I sometimes got confused. My mind didn't work right for awhile. I kept thinking about your mother being hit every time a baby was about to be delivered. I don't know why."

Taking off his glasses, he rubbed his eyes. They were a steely gray, but gentle. For the first time Crista realized how gentle her father must look to others— like a big teddy bear. He shook his head and sighed again. "There was a bad situation. A breech birth. We had to make some fast decisions. Then we discovered the baby was strangling—tied up in the umbilical chord. For some reason..."

His voice was hard now, cracking, breaking.

"For some reason I froze. I just froze. The image of you and your mother kept clogging my brain. I couldn't see right. I almost fainted. My delay..."

He lay back. The emotion was obvious. Crista leaned forward, her eyes not straying from his face.

"My delay almost lost that baby's life. Thank God it was all right. No one even said it was my fault. But I knew. The next day I decided to go into general practice."

There was a long silence.

"So you won't ever deliver babies again?"

Dr. Mayfield nodded. "I don't know whether I can, Honey. Even now sometimes... Your mother was the best thing that ever happened to me."

Suddenly Crista was crying. "I'm so sorry, Daddy. It was all my fault. I was playing around. Mom saved me, but I killed her. I killed my own mother." Her chest heaved and she felt as if a weight had fallen onto her back, crumpling her into a tight ball.

She was barely aware that he was staring at her, but then he moved toward her. Instinctively she stood up at the same time. "Daddy, I'm so sorry. I should never..."

Instantly they were in each other's arms. "Crista," he said, "it was an accident. It was a crazy, happenstance accident. It could have happened to anybody. It was never your fault."

"But, Daddy, I was teasing Mom and we had been arguing about clothes or something..."

His voice was fierce and strong. "Crista, you were 11 years old. You didn't cause anything to happen. The man was drunk!"

As they held one another, she felt his chest trembling. He whispered, "Have you thought all this time it was your fault?"

She brushed at the tears. "But I was in the street. I didn't look. I shouldn't have been..."

He looked at her with alarm. "You weren't in the street, Crista."

Her heart almost stopped. "I wasn't?"

"Your mother and you were on the sidewalk, waiting to cross. The drunk driver lost control of his car as it rushed down toward you. Your mother just had time to push you out of the way. If it was anyone's fault, it was his."

Crista stared at him, astonished. "But I thought . . ."

Her father crushed her in his arms. "Have you thought all this time it was your fault?"

She wept in his arms and shook her head. "I thought you hated me."

Their bodies quaked against one another. For a long time they stood there, not moving. Then he released her and wiped his eyes. "We should have talked. I'm so sorry. I just didn't know you felt that way."

She looked into his eyes. "Do you still have all the pictures?"

He grimaced, then nodded. "Yes."

"Let's look at them. Together."

Suddenly they were like two little kids on Christmas morning. He retrieved the photo albums from the hiding place in the cellar and they looked through them, weeping over old memories, smiling at Mrs. Mayfield caught in different poses.

After an hour of the closeness, Crista said, "You loved her a lot, didn't you, Daddy?"

"We both did, Honey."

"But we'll see her again, won't we?"

"That's what the Bible teaches."

This time they prayed together in the living room before the roaring fire. It was a wonderful moment for Crista, and for the first time she realized the dam had broken. They were father and daughter again.

For a long time that night she lay quiet in her room thinking. In a way, she hoped her father would go back to delivering babies. But she knew she certainly couldn't make him. She thought how nice it would be if he had been Nadine's doctor.

But that was another problem. Before she fell asleep she prayed again, "Please, God, let everything work out for Nadine and Johnny." The next thing she knew it was 7 A.M. and her alarm was clanging away on her dresser.

·20·
Stuck

Snow had come on Thanksgiving and several times in early December. Crista hauled out her snowshoes and trekked through the woods to the Semms, helping Nadine make a pie on one occasion and staying for an early dinner one night when her father planned on coming home late.

Then there was a heavy snow on December 15— nearly 20 inches. Crista wasn't sure whether she should be worried about the coming of the baby or just excited. She knew she was a little of each. Nadine looked like she might pop any minute. She often lay on her bed moaning. More than once Crista gave her a back rub and helped her stagger around the living room to soothe the swelling in her legs.

Still, Nadine would not discuss a doctor with Crista. It was clear she felt confident all would be well. They had everything prepared and ready. A table by the baby's crib was laid out with surgical scissors, gauze, and most of the implements of delivery. Three books stood between the two glass bookends on a shelf that Johnny had recently put up.

Johnny tried to persuade Nadine to change her mind about the doctor, twice in Crista's presence. But Nadine argued that they had no health insurance or savings, and the two doctors she had checked out had sent her to a Social Services clinic in Honesdale. Nadine yelled, "I'm not being any charity case!"

Crista prayed about it every time she remembered—in school, during lunch, after recess, before recess, on the bus on the way home, while walking the trails. Even Rontu and Tigger seemed to realize something was up as they panted after her on the treks through the woods.

A heavy snowstorm hit on December 20, a Friday. The woods were crammed full and the snow was so light that the snowshoes sank nearly a foot before squeaking to a stop. Crista tromped through the forest that afternoon while it was still snowing, exhausted and sweating through her underclothes. She had been up late the last three nights working on some more art projects. With school finishing up, plus the daily visits to Nadine and Johnny and her own chores around the house, Crista was dead tired. But she knew she couldn't desert her friends. Not now. Not when the baby was so close.

Rontu and Tigger greeted Crista each day at the midpoint of the trail by The Love Tree. Tigger's tail rapped against Crista's boots, leaving an angel-wing swirl in the snow. Rontu was equally happy, giving her several deep-throated woofs that made a few close boughs drop their snow in a great shush. Both dogs sank deep in the snow, Tigger up to his chest, but they had learned that following Crista's snowshoed tracks made the going a lot easier.

The snow fell in chunky snowflakes, stuck together on the way down through the cold air. Crista's breath came in great heaves as she wallowed up the trail. In a way, all she wanted to do was sleep. But she told herself to stay just a short time, see how things were, and then go home.

When she arrived at the Semms, Johnny was hauling in firewood.

"I'd wave, but I have to get in this timber," he yelled as he opened the front door with his foot.

Crista hurried up. "I'll hold it for you." She stripped her boots out of the snowshoes and jumped onto the porch. The two dogs lay down in two barren spots on the porch where the wind had blown the snow away.

Johnny stopped her before going in. "She's not doing well, Crista. I hope this goes okay."

Crista grimaced, then waited as he went inside. A roaring fire greeted them with playful laps of its flaming fingers. Boiling water steamed on the gas stove. A wreath hung over the fireplace with a huge red bow and pine cones attached. Crista had helped Nadine make it a week before. Candles flickered in the windows, rooted to the sill by melted but now hardened wax. Johnny was trying to save gas for the electric generator so that they would have it in an emergency.

Nadine moaned from the bedroom, "I was hoping you'd come."

"How are you doing?" One look told Crista not well. She pulled off her mittens, cap, and coat and hung them in the pegs on the other side of the bedroom door.

"I just wish it would be over." Nadine's face was puffy and white. Her usually rosy cheeks looked pallid, almost pasty. "I've been so cooped up in this cabin that maybe a visit to the hospital wouldn't be so bad."

The wind rattled snow against the windowpanes.

"Oh, feel!" Nadine said. "He's kicking!" She placed Crista's hand flat on her belly.

Crista smiled. "He's got big legs. Or she." The baby felt all knotted up inside, but she could feel a little hardness that she imagined might be a knee or elbow.

"He," Nadine said. "The size of this guy has to be a he." Nadine looked up into Crista's eyes. "I'm glad you came. It'll be any day now."

Sometimes Crista wasn't even sure why she came every day. She dreaded the thought of the baby coming while she was there. In a way she just wanted to show up some afternoon and learn the baby had arrived the night before.

Crista made some tea and they drank it together, with a little sugar. Nadine liked something called "SleepyTime Tea," and it was always refreshing, with the scent of herbs and spices spiraling in steam into the air.

After the tea, Nadine closed her eyes and began to fall asleep. The days had been long and hard. With all the activity in getting ready, both Johnny and Nadine were exhausted. Johnny collapsed onto the couch in the living room after letting the dogs inside. In a few minutes he was lightly snoring. Rontu and Tigger curled up in front of the fire.

Crista sat at the table, chiding herself to get up and get home.

But the thick, warm air of the cabin caressed her face and back. She laid her head down on the table. The clock ticked on the mantel. The last she heard was the five bongs at five in the afternoon.

The next thing Crista knew Johnny was patting her back. "Crista! Crista! Wake up. It's past ten o'clock."

Crista turned a sleepy face toward the voice. "What?"

"Ten o'clock." Johnny murmured unhappily under his breath. "I'm sorry. I really conked out. Everybody did. Nadine's still asleep."

The two dogs lay on the big mat inside the door. They both stood, wagging their tails as Crista got up.

"I'll have to drive you home," Johnny said. "It must have snowed ten inches while we were out."

They both stared out the window. Crista rubbed at the frosty pane. "The truck's completely covered."

Johnny sighed noisily. "It's got big tires. We should be able to get down the mountain. I didn't know it got this deep up here."

Nadine stirred on the bed behind them. Crista and Johnny turned to look at her. Nadine's eyes opened and she gazed at them sleepily. She stretched, sending her arms out and turning them. "I feel so good," she said.

"You ought to," Johnny said. "We were out like lights. We've all been asleep more than five hours."

Nadine rubbed her eyes. "Crista, your father..."

"I know," Crista moaned. "He'll kill me. He doesn't even know I'm here."

"I'm taking you home," Johnny said. "That's all there is to it. Let's get it done right away. I want to be back here as soon as possible."

Crista shook her head. "I can go through the woods."

Again, Johnny shook his head fiercely. "Do you have a flashlight? My batteries are almost gone. I meant to get some new ones this afternoon. It won't provide much light."

"I forgot mine."

"Then we're going in the truck. You be okay, Nadine?"

Nadine sat up, groaning. "I don't think he wants to come out tonight. You'd better get her down there."

Johnny and Crista dressed for the outside and opened the door. Snow blew in, throwing napkins on the floor and lobbing bits of snow all over the living room. Nadine hugged her shoulders. "Hurry up!"

Johnny and Crista slipped out. She picked up her snowshoes leaning up against the front of the house on the porch. Johnny told the dogs to wait inside and keep Nadine company. Then he and Crista cleaned off the truck. She threw her snowshoes in the back and jumped into the cab.

"You sure this will get through?" she asked nervously. "That snow is over 20 inches in some places. And there are probably drifts, with this wind."

Johnny smiled, "This little four-wheel road-eater will go through anything."

He fired up the engine and pulled out of the yard, spinning the tires and making a sidewinding arc in the snow. He worked the truck quickly into the barely visible impressions of the track. His lights cut the night and the snow clattered down around them in ticks and sprays. The windshield wipers clacked back and forth. The rear wheels spun and Johnny shoved the lever into four-wheel drive. He opened his side window and snow whooshed in.

"Open your window so I can see on the side," he called. Crista cranked the handle.

"Now watch this," he called above the roar of the wind. "This rockin' bird is gonna fly."

The big tires dug in and heaved the truck forward. Crista gritted her teeth, praying in her mind that they would get home in one piece and then Johnny would make it back up. The truck seemed to know intuitively where the track was. They hurtled down the trail like a boat through water.

"Be careful!" Crista yelled.

"It's okay. This thing is like a tank."

Wind blew sheets of snow against the windshield. Johnny hit the brakes and slowed down, spinning the wheel as the road veered to the left and then to the right. "We'll be passing the dump soon," he hollered.

The smell of smoke from the dump sifted into their nostrils. The truck skidded back and forth at about 20 miles an hour. Crista felt it was too fast, but she knew the machine was acting more like a snowmobile than a truck. She looked to her right and saw the pit of the dump and the falloff over the edge.

Then the truck hit a huge bump.

"Doggone, I knew about that rock," Johnny said with aggravation.

The truck swiveled left and the rear came around. "Just hold on!" Johnny cried.

The truck fishtailed and hit another bump. This time both Johnny and Crista hit the ceiling with their heads. Johnny jerked the wheel and hit the brakes. "We're out of the track."

The whole back came around and banged into a huge rock off the edge of the trail. The truck crunched to a sickening stop. The rear end had slipped over the edge of the trail opposite the dump and its nose pointed into the air slightly.

Johnny murmured something Crista didn't understand.

"I can't get out," he said. "I'm right up against the rock."

Crista looked out the window. "I think it's okay over here."

They both got out and inspected the truck. Johnny waded around it in the snow. "You know how to use a clutch?"

Crista shook her head.

"Okay, I'll have to get in the cab. You see what you can do to push."

Swishing through the snow to the back of the truck, Crista called out, "Go ahead."

He hit the gas. The wheels spun, hurling snow and dirt back at Crista. She threw her weight into the truck, but it wasn't much. The front tires spun on the snow and the back ones couldn't get a bite. The truck rocked, but only slid further into the ditch.

Johnny yelled, "When I say, 'Go,' push at the same time."

They tried that. It got nowhere. Within five minutes they were both sweating and panting.

"It's stuck," Crista said meekly.

Johnny blew white puffs of breath into the air. The snow kept falling. Already the top of the truck was covered and the windshield was filling up.

"What should we do?" Johnny asked. "It'll take us an hour to get back to the house. Maybe you should just go around on your showshoes."

Crista shook her head. "I don't know this trail. And the dump dogs might be around. I think we should go back. I'll just have to wait till the snow stops."

In the light of the cab, Johnny looked angry and frustrated. "I'm sorry, Crista. Your dad's gonna be mad, huh?"

"He'll be all right. He's been real good lately." But in her heart, Crista worried that he would be upset she was missing. He would have no idea where she was.

She took out the snowshoes. "Do you want to wear them?"

"No, I'll be all right. Put them on. Let's just stick together. I do have a .22 target pistol in the truck. I'll get it out. And the flashlight."

Johnny fumbled around under the seat and put the pistol inside his jacket. "Well, let's hit it." He clicked on the light a moment. It was dim, but it would help. He turned it off right away, though. "We should save it."

They began the long climb back up the mountain. As they started off, Crista looked at her watch in the last light of the cab before they closed the door— 11:15. Her father would give it to her for sure.

Sweat slipped down her armpit. The road was pitch black. Only because two deep lines cut it in the middle where the truck drove could they find the path at all. The snow kept falling and falling and falling.

Johnny lugged behind her, thrashing through the snow. Even with snowshoes, the going was tough. Crista thought if she had to raise her leg one more time she would die.

But soon they saw the light of the cabin ahead. It was past 12:30 when they lumbered into the yard. The wind screeched above them. Snow slashed at her face. Her cheeks felt thin and raw as paper. As they neared the cabin, though, they heard Nadine.

"Yiiiiii!"

Both of them stood still. A terror gripped Crista. Then Johnny stumbled on ahead and reached the cabin ahead of Crista. Snow blocked the door, but he raked back the snow with his gloves. As he did, two more "Yiiii's" slit the night.

When the light of the cabin glowed open, Nadine yelled, "Johnny, I'm in labor. The baby is coming."

·21·
Help!

Crista froze in the doorway. Her snowshoes clattered on the porch as they fell down from the place where she tried to lean them. Both dogs barked.

When she stepped into the warmth of the cabin, she could see Nadine's face white with fright. She stood in the middle of it in her nightshirt, squatting and stumbling about. "Where's the truck?"

"Stuck," Johnny said, ripping off his coat. "How are you?"

"The contractions are about every eight minutes. I...Yiiiii!" Nadine's lips contorted and she closed her eyes. Johnny rushed to her side. Crista stared.

Nadine wheezed, "Man, that hurts. I didn't know it would be this bad." She was breathing hard. She stood, pressing her hand into her back.

"We've got to do that breathing stuff," Johnny said. "Like the book said."

Squeezing her eyes shut, Nadine breathed steadily. "It hurts bad, Johnny. It's really bad. Maybe we should have gone for that..."

Johnny shook his head. "It's too late for that now." He said to Crista, "She's supposed to have ice. I think

189

we can use icicles from the house, or just a panful of snow. Could you get some?"

Crista nodded dumbly, her heart hammering. Rontu licked her exposed hand and she gave him a quick caress. She grabbed the pan from the table with all the supplies and went outside with the dogs. She scooped up a pile of snow, then came back in. Rontu and Tigger disappeared into the darkness.

Nadine screamed again and Crista froze. *She'll never make it*, she thought. *We need a doctor!*

She jerked open the door and hurried back in with the snow. Johnny was frantically gathering things on the table. "The baby won't be ready till your things..."

"Contractions." Nadine groaned out the word like a slow curse.

"Contractions are like a minute apart or less, right?"

"I have to go all the way down to that?"

Crista looked from Johnny to Nadine.

"You read the book," Johnny screeched. "Nadine, you wanted to do this."

"I didn't know it would be like this." She leaned on the table, panting, her face wet with sweat.

"It'll be okay," Johnny said, glancing at Crista, his brow wrinkled, his face white with terror. "We can't go for a doctor now, Nadine."

Nadine stumbled toward the bedroom. Her grimace soon turned into an agonized contortion. "I can't stand it!" she cried as she stood shaking in the doorway. "Ayyyyyy!"

Crista couldn't move. She looked from Johnny to Nadine and back to Johnny. He seemed rooted to his spot, halfway between the table and the bedroom. He turned to her, "Do you know anything about this, Crista? I feel like my mind's just flown the coop."

Somehow Crista pushed her feet toward Nadine. "I think the first thing is we have to make sure the baby's pointed in the right direction." How she remembered that, she didn't know. But it came to her.

As Johnny stepped back, Nadine climbed onto the bed and lay back, wiping her brow with a towel, then pulling up a sheet.

Johnny said, "I think I should just..." He turned away.

A chilly burr ran up Crista's spine. He wanted her to do this?

Johnny gave her a guilty nod and waited.

Crista touched Nadine's belly through the sheet. It felt hard, taut, like you could bounce a ball on it. Nadine pushed back the sheet. "Feel and see if it feels right," she gasped.

Her throat dry, Crista moved her hands over the stiff, almost rigid surface. A hardness seemed to move under her hands, but she had no idea what part of the baby it could be. The head? The rear end? A shoulder? She knew the baby had to get into a headfirst position or it would be a breech birth and that would be big trouble. But she couldn't figure out where the head was.

"Yiiii! Oh, that hurts!" Nadine shrieked for ten seconds, and pulled her legs up, then rolled on her side in pain. "Johnny, help me!" She stopped with a sudden suck of air.

Crista caressed her side, searching for words of encouragement.

The air grew still as everyone waited. Johnny looked at his watch, his face white with panic, his hair matted and wet. "Six and three-quarters minutes apart."

"You have to do those breathing things," Crista said, trying to sound confident. She had read in one of her father's books how breathing in certain patterns sometimes helped.

Johnny stepped over to the side of the bed. "Right, remember—in, out, in, out, in, in, out, out—all that."

Nadine waved her hand back to Johnny, her back still facing them. "Hold my hand, just hold my hand."

"In, Nadine," Johnny said. "In, in, in. Breathe in. Then out." He began making huffing noises. He motioned to Crista and she imitated him. The two of them breathed loudly and Nadine caught the rhythm.

Then the contraction hit.

"In-out, in-out, in-out," Johnny yelled.

Nadine grabbed Crista's hand with her free hand. Her squeeze almost broke Crista's fingers. But somehow she managed to breathe in unison. When the pain passed, she lay back on the pillow, swallowing hard. "That wasn't as bad."

Another hour passed with the contractions staying about six minutes apart.

For two more hours, Johnny and Crista sat by the side of the bed, watching, fighting off the urge to sleep.

Then Nadine screamed. Really screamed. "This is pain, Johnny. Oh, this is pain." The contractions were still only five minutes apart. Crista caressed Nadine's belly again.

It was then that she saw the blood. Underneath Nadine on the white sheets.

"You're bleeding!" Crista cried. "You're bleeding, Nadine. Bad."

Nadine felt with her hand, then stared at the redness on her fingers. "What does that mean? Could something be wrong with the baby?"

Crista swallowed. She had no idea. They needed a doctor. This was wrong. All wrong. She had to get a doctor. Someone. *Daddy!* But what if he...? Could he...?

She didn't finish the question. Suddenly, she said firmly, "I'm going for my father."

Nadine stared at her. But before she could protest, another contraction hit. She shrieked. Johnny gripped her hand, trying to get her to breathe in unison.

"I should go," he yelled in desperation as he looked at the blood.

Crista shook her head, already pulling on her coat. "I can do it. I know the way. I have the snowshoes. And you know how to help with the breathing. It's got to be me. Where's the flashlight?"

Johnny closed his eyes, still gripping Nadine's hand. "I'm sorry, Crissie. I should never have let this happen. Are you sure?"

"Where's the flashlight?"

He pointed to the table where he had left it. "You'll be all right?"

Crista nodded, suddenly feeling like she was hurling herself out onto a raging sea.

Nadine forced out a sentence with a gasp. "We don't have insur..."

Immediately Johnny shook his head angrily. "We need a doctor, Nay. We should never have tried this. Now we're in trouble..."

Hunching forward, Nadine bunched her fists. The contraction struck just as she began to shake her head. "Ahhhhhh!"

Crista grabbed her mittens and hat. By the time she was ready, Nadine lay back on the bed, panting and throbbing. Her eyes were squeezed shut. Crista fled out the door.

"Daddy," she murmured as she knelt to tie on the snowshoes. "I know Daddy will help. He's got to. He's the only one. He won't say no."

·22·

The Forest

The snow bit Crista's cheeks. The darkness looked hard and terrible. Still, the sky had cleared a bit. Behind the thick clouds a blue moon poked now and then. Rontu and Tigger weren't in the yard, but she sensed that they might be near. She tramped up toward the trail, able to spot the cut in the trees even in the dark.

The silence of the woods was overpowering. Snow trickled through the leaves and pine needles like parachuting angels. The wind had died down. It was only her and the eerie silence of a snow-filled wood. It made her think of a poem they had read that year by Robert Frost. "Whose woods these are I think I know..." That was all she could remember. Then the end, "And miles to go before I sleep. Miles to go before I sleep."

Miles, she thought. How far was it? How long would it take? How long could Nadine hold out?

She prayed silently as she walked. *Please, God, let me make it.*

As she stepped away from the light of the cabin, she peered at her watch one last time: 5:00 A.m. It would be dawn soon. She felt like she could fall down in a hump and sleep right in the middle of the trail.

The trees towered over her. In the darkness, she could feel their feathery stillness and nearness. But the trail? Even with the trees parted slightly at the point near the cabin, she strained to see where she was going in the dark. She turned on the flashlight momentarily to see where the tree was. She could see the four-foot-wide space between the trees. But with the snow, it seemed impossible. Everything looked the same. It made her feel as if she was inside a monstrous unlit cave. The silence sent prickles of fear up and down her back. She sensed that her forehead and her hands were sweating. She turned off the flashlight. "Got to save it," she told herself.

She bumped into boughs. Branches grabbed at her parka and sent showers of snow onto her face, down her neck. The sudden cold made her shiver. Where was she going?

Please, God ... Nadine needs help. Please don't let anything happen....

She pressed on, forcing herself to believe she was going the right way. The first strips of gray appeared in the sky in the distance. Soon the sun would rise. That would help.

She pushed on. A half-hour passed. Forty-five minutes. She flashed the light on her watch just to make sure. But all sense of time was gone. She couldn't tell the trail from the forest. Even in good weather, it was only a track, barely two waists wide. She looked back and forth, searching the trees for a sign of something familiar. Suddenly she realized how easy a trail was— when you could see it—and how scary the woods were without one. Her bearings were gone. She didn't even know which way the cabin was.

Tears burned into her eyes as she frantically searched for the way. She stood in a slight clearing straining to hear a sound—the highway, anything. Every direction looked the same. The darkness seemed to close in on her. The falling snow made the silence even more eerie.

She flashed the light on again and searched around. It was dim. She knew the batteries wouldn't last much longer.

Then she saw a track to her left. She hurried toward it, the shoes making a swishing noise and then a squeak as it settled five or six inches into the snow. She turned the light on the track. What was it? Snowshoes? Maybe there was someone else out here.

She called out, "Hello! Anyone there?"

She waited. No answer.

"HELLO!"

Nothing.

She flashed the light on the track ahead, then on her own trail behind her. "It's my own track!" she cried suddenly. "I'm going in circles!"

She stifled a cry. She prided herself on her ability in the woods, but with the snow every instinct had vanished.

Please, God. Please!

She pushed away from the tracks, thinking she had to run into something familiar. It was getting lighter now, and hopefully she would soon see something she recognized.

Then she heard barking. Dump dogs?

"Rontu!" she screamed. "Please be Rontu!"

A low woof answered her. She shone the light in the direction. Two blue eyes appeared, almost shrouded in snow. He was up to his haunches in it.

A moment later, the big dog surged through the snow and nuzzled her mittened hand. Behind him leaped Tigger, like a boy stepping stones across a stream.

She knelt down, hugging them with relief. "Boy, am I glad to see you!" She gripped Rontu's neck as he panted happily. Then she stood up. "Look, I need your help, guys. You have to show me the trail out to the road. To the road, Rontu. Tigger, you too. Do you understand? I need to find the road." She made a sound like a car.

Rontu's tail wagged. Tigger barked.

"The road," Crista said again. "The lake. Where the lake is." She waved her arms.

Rontu cocked his head. "You have to lead me to the highway. I have to get to home. HOME!"

Suddenly Rontu barked and turned around. Both dogs bounded forward.

She clumped through the woods after them. The first vague scabs of gray came into the sky. Rontu leaped and hurdled through the snow like a horse in a steeplechase. Both dogs turned and looked back at her momentarily, then bounded ahead.

She still hadn't reached the trail. Did they understand? She shone the light but recognized nothing.

Then they stopped in front of a tree, panting and staring at her. Crista stomped up to them, her face sweaty, her breathing heavy. It was nowhere. They didn't understand. They were as lost as she was.

But Rontu nipped his nose in the direction of the tree. Crista stared at it, then turned on the light. A cry came into her throat. It was The Love Tree. She blinked with thanks. Even the initials on it were visible with flecks of snow caught in the crevices.

"You did understand," she cried, patting Rontu and Tigger together. "At least as best you could." They wagged their tails happily. Rontu woofed.

Crista turned around, getting her bearings. Yes, she could see the trail now. The snow on it was fresh, though Rontu or another dog had crossed it once or twice. Elbow Rock had to be about 200 yards ahead on the left. She recognized the other signs, a big fir and another clump of pines.

"I know where I am!" she cried. "I know. Come on."

Both dogs barked. She lurched forward. With the growing gray in the sky and the sun starting to shine gold far to her left, the east, it was easier now. In the distance she heard the whir of a snowmobile engine and wondered who might be out. Could she find them? Were they neighbors?

The dogs leaped and rested, leaped and rested ahead of her through the deep snow. They would be at Elbow Rock any minute.

Then more barking. Dump dogs, she thought. It had to be.

Don't let them come this way, she murmured, then pressed on. The two dogs were far ahead of her now, but they were going the right way. Now she could see Elbow Rock, a huge pile of snow on top of it like thick vanilla frosting on a wedding cake.

As she worked her way down, she saw more tracks in the snow—snowshoes and boot tracks. Some people had been here, perhaps less than an hour before. What would they be doing?

She stopped and stared at the tracks a moment. Suddenly she realized her father had probably called the police, maybe an ambulance. He might even have had searchers out looking for her.

Crista swallowed and hurried along. Her coat felt damp inside. She didn't feel the cold now at all, but her heart hammered.

The dogs barked ahead of her. *Please don't let him be mad,* she thought. But her fear for Nadine took over and she gritted her teeth. *I have to get there. That's all that matters.*

A moment later there was a loud report: BOOM!

A gunshot! her mind cried.

Snow fell off boughs. Crista stumbled forward, then knelt with fear.

Someone firing a gun. She flicked on the flashlight. "Don't shoot!" she called.

A voice yelled back. "Watch out, there're two dogs here."

Rontu and Tigger.

Crista jumped up. "Don't shoot them. They're mine."

There was a silence. Then, "Who are you?"

"Crista! Crista Mayfield!"

Whoever it was cheered. "Thank God! We've been looking for you for hours!"

Crista hurried around a drift and saw the man, the two dogs crouching in the snow and panting. He wore a thick Russian-style cap with a badge in the front. His blue parka also bristled a silver badge.

"Are you all right?" He yelled. He shone a flashlight into her eyes. She winced, then shook her head, stepping forward.

"Yes. I'm fine. I'm sorry. Some people..." She stopped. She felt as if she wanted to crumple into a ball and go to sleep.

The policeman wore high hunting boots. He waded toward her. "Come on. The road is just ahead. Your father thought you were attacked by dogs or something. The dogs out here are crazy. These are yours?"

Crista patted Rontu on the head. "They helped me find my way."

The officer smiled grimly. "All right. Then let's get you home."

He waved her toward the freshly plowed road, extending his hand. "We've had two search teams out for hours."

In several minutes they reached the road. The two dogs stood on the edge of the clearing. It was past 7:00 A.M. The first bright red of morning gleamed on the horizon. The clouds were clearing and the snow had slowed to flurries. There was over 30 inches on the ground, and in many places huge drifts. Without the snowshoes she wouldn't have made a hundred yards. A plow roared by on the highway, casting a wake of snow on the side of the road.

In front of the dogs she spotted the treaded, triple track of a snowmobile. She stood shivering, gazing at the slope of snow left by the plow. The policeman climbed up the huge bank left by the plow. He sank in deep. But he held out his hand. "You should take off your snowshoes to cross the road."

She climbed up. The dogs started to climb with her, but without snowshoes they just sank deeper into the loose snow.

"It'll be okay," she told them. "Wait here."

As she poked her head over the top, she saw the road. She had really made it.

Immediately she remembered Nadine. She touched the policeman's arm as she looked back and forth along the highway. "Please. There're some friends. In the woods. She's having a baby. They need a doctor. She's in labor now. They're at a hunting cabin."

The policeman grabbed her at the shoulder, not paying attention to her, but watching the road. "Okay, there's no second plow. Let's just get you down to the house. The other team is there."

Crista grasped his arm. "Please. My friends need a doctor. They need my father. She's having a baby. Right now."

The officer stared at her. "There's someone out there having a baby?" He had thin red cheeks, but friendly green eyes.

Crista nodded briskly.

His mouth dropped.

"All right," he said suddenly. "We'll take care of it. We have some snowmobiles. Let's let everyone know you're found first." He stared off into the woods and shook his head with wonder. His breath came in white chuffs.

Crista held the officer's arm as they tramped across the road. Rontu and Tigger leaped across ahead of them.

When they reached the Mayfield cabin, three snowmobiles sat in the road, steam rising off them. Crista swallowed back her fear, praying that her father wouldn't be too angry. She pulled off her snowshoes again at the top of the walk.

She turned to the police officer. "Do you think my father..."

Before she finished the sentence, she heard a cry behind her. Her father ran out of the house in his plaid hunting shirt. "Crista! Crista! Baby!"

Crista turned and leaped into his arms.

He kissed her. His eyes were wet. "I thought you'd frozen in the woods or were lost or the dogs got you." His hug was tight and warm. His breath smelled of coffee and a pipe.

Several other policemen hurried out of the house, cheering. One went to a snowmobile and started talking on a radio.

"Where were you? I was frantic."

Her voice trembled, but she got out the words quickly. "There're some people who live in a cabin. The old hunting cabin. I visit them a lot. She's pregnant. We all fell asleep at the house yesterday afternoon and when we got up it was past ten. I was terrified. We tried to get home. But the truck went into a ditch."

Officer Manlon, the man who had first spoken to Crista, came over. "That must have been the pickup we saw near the dump. We just thought it was someone leaving trash."

Crista nodded. "Then we had to go back to the cabin. And when we got back, Nadine was in labor. Please, Daddy, we have to hurry. I should have told you before. But she needs help. They're poor. They don't have a doctor. They had reasons, but now . . ." Crista's eyes burned with tears.

Her father searched her eyes. "A woman having a baby? Now?" He shook his head in anger and wonder.

Blinking back the tears, Crista said, "Remember the pregnant lady at the art awards?"

"Vaguely."

"They . . . I don't know. Please. Can you go? Now? They need a doctor. The baby's stuck, I think. Please." She remembered what he had said when he told her he couldn't deliver another baby.

Dr. Mayfield's eyes flickered with pain and fear. Then he turned to the policemen. "Can we use the snowmobiles?"

Officer Manlon nodded. "Saddle up, men. We're going to deliver a baby."

·23·

Fairlight and More

"You'll have to show us the way," the sergeant said. "Can you do it?" He looked from Crista to Dr. Mayfield.

Her father nodded, putting Crista down on the ground in her boots. "Let me get my bag and some instruments. No one else is close enough. If the baby is breech, it could be real trouble." He turned to Crista. "You can show us the way? You're not too tired?"

Relief like a rush crackled through her chest. "Yes. I know it perfectly. The trail should be all marked by my tracks, anyway."

Dr. Mayfield went inside. The policemen started up their machines. A few minutes later Dr. Mayfield appeared with his black bag. He wore the red plaid hunting coat and a cap.

Officer Manlon organized the men. "You'll have to go on the lead vehicle," he said to Crista. "Behind Private Lutts." A tall thin man waved from the lead snowmobile. Crista clambered on behind him.

A moment later Dr. Mayfield got on with Officer Manlon. Two other officers jumped onto the third machine. With a roar, they all turned around and headed up the road. The dogs leaped behind them, following stoutly.

The rush of air felt good on her hot face. Crista directed Private Lutts through the woods. In a matter of what seemed only minutes, they buzzed into the yard at the cabin. Johnny was already running out the door when they turned off the machines.

"We've got the whole police force!" Crista cried. "And my father."

Johnny's eyes were wide with hope as he led the men in "Less than a minute apart and she's really hurtin', Dr. Mayfield. I'm sorry. But we..."

Crista's father hurried past him to Nadine's bed, where she lay with her legs bent and up. There was a towel in her mouth. He gave some quick orders to the men, asked Johnny to stoke up the fire, and called Crista to his side. Nadine's eyes blinked with terror as the pain struck. Dr. Mayfield put on rubber gloves and made a quick examination.

"Okay, she's close," he said. "Almost ten centimeters. Luckily, it's not breech."

He called Johnny over. "I want you to hold your wife's hand, and when I tell her to push, I want you to push with her. Encourage her. Got it?"

Johnny nodded his head fiercely, then turned to look at Nadine. Her eyes were shut tight with pain and her mouth emitted cries through the cloth.

Turning to Crista, Dr. Mayfield said, "Honey, I have to administer an anesthetic. I may have to cut her. You'll have to be my nurse. You can't get emotional now." He handed her a pair of rubber gloves. "Put these on."

She followed his directions. He handed her a pair of bent medical pliers with a wad of gauze caught between the jaws. He showed her where to position it.

"When she starts bleeding—if I have to cut her—I hope I don't—you have to hold this on the incision. Then when the baby comes, I want you to continue holding it in place."

Nadine yelled in pain, but Johnny gripped her hand and told her to be strong. Dr. Mayfield examined Nadine again. "All right, I'm going to give you a shot of painkiller. Just think about skiing down a mountain."

Grimacing, Nadine yelled again as the contraction hit. Dr. Mayfield gave her the shot.

Moments later he pulled out a scalpel. "Just a minute or two. We only need a few minutes."

Four more times Nadine screamed as the contractions hit. Crista held the gauze in position. She didn't know whether to shriek or weep. Dr. Mayfield examined Nadine again. "Ten centimeters," he said. "I can see a head."

Crista could see it too. Brown hair slicked down. Round.

The doctor said to Nadine, "Push, girl, push with all your might."

The head moved, got bigger, filled the space. Then there was the face, the neck, the tiny hunched shoulders. A moment later the whole baby slid into Dr. Mayfield's palms. "It's a girl!" he cried. Crista noticed the tears in his eyes as he worked. He seemed in complete control. If he was having the problems he had before, he didn't show it. Crista prayed as he worked. Her eyes smarted with tears. But she held the gauze in place.

She peered at the tiny form barely filling Dr. Mayfield's hands. The face looked all right, though wrinkly and red. *That small and Nadine's belly so big? How could it be?* Her father cleaned out its mouth, then pinched its bottom. A crisp cry broke from the baby's mouth as it took its first breath. Crista's heart felt as though it would zing out of her body and smash into the ceiling with joy.

Dr. Mayfield tied off the umbilical cord and wrapped the baby in a towel. He handed her to Johnny. "Hold her there, son. Just for a minute."

Nadine continued to look in pain. More contractions came. She cried twice and breathed rapidly. She squeezed her eyes tight like she didn't even realize what had happened.

"All right," Dr. Mayfield said. "Here comes the second one."

Crista looked up astonished. Johnny's jaw dropped. "The second one!"

Dr. Mayfield looked up from his examination. "Yes, two. Twins!" He smiled. "I guess you didn't know." He was grinning.

Crista felt as though her heart would leap out of her chest. Her father was grinning. She had never seen him grin like that before.

The mother concentrated, her brow wrinkled, as if still unaware of all that was going on. Moments later, another brown tousle-haired head appeared. Then shoulders. This time it was a boy. Crista watched her father remove white and gray mucus from the baby's throat. A fractured cry cut the quiet.

Johnny's blue eyes were popping out. "Two! Twins,

Nadine. We had twins." He looked around at Dr. May-field and said with a tremble, "Are there any more in there?"

Shaking his head, Dr. Mayfield joked, "That's the end of the show, folks."

Nadine opened her eyes wide. For the first time in hours, she smiled. "Let me hold them, Honey."

Johnny handed her the first baby clumsily. Nadine nestled her in the crook of her arm. Dr. Mayfield finished with the second baby, wrapped him up, and handed him to Johnny. He gave Nadine a quick exam-ination. "No, I'm afraid there're definitely no more coming out today." He touched Crista's bare arm and laughed.

Nadine's eyes teared. "They're so beautiful," she said. "The girl's name is Rebekah—Rebekah Fairlight Crista. And the boy..."

"John, Junior," Johnny said triumphantly.

"Johnny, Junior," Nadine said. She winked at Cri-sta. Her face streamed with sweat. She looked like she would collapse any second. But her eyes glowed with joy.

Dr. Mayfield finished up with the afterbirth and gave Nadine a final examination. Then he went out to tell the policemen on the porch. They began beeping their snowmobiles and one radioed to the station. "It's a girl and a boy!" Crista heard Sergeant Manlon yell into the microphone. They told the whole story to their comrades in town.

Nadine let Crista hold each of them as she rocked the other in her arms. As Crista held Fairlight, the baby gurgled. Her eyes stayed closed, but suddenly Crista felt joy like a geyser shoot through her. She

looked up at her father. He smiled at her proudly—
that smile she had seen so long ago. And it was for her.
Then he gave her a kiss. "I'm proud of you, Honey. You
did great. You'll have to do another painting."

A lump crowded Crista's throat. She wanted to hug
him, but she basked in the radiance of his smile like a
beautiful model sunning on the beach.

Dr. Mayfield said to Johnny, "I think you two should
consider coming to our house for a few days. This is no
place for newborns. At least for awhile. If you can't go
to the hospital, that's the next best thing."

Johnny turned to Nadine. "What do you think,
Nay?"

Sergeant Manlon stood brushing off snow in the
doorway.

"How would we get there?"

Sergeant Manlon boomed, "We can arrange that."

Even Nadine laughed.

•   •   •

Sergeant Manlon took the Semms and their babies
down the mountain in a Snow Caterpillar. In the afternoon, Dr. Mayfield cornered Crista in their kitchen as
Johnny settled Nadine and the babies in a bed in the
guestroom.

"So this was your secret," her father said, "a family,
and a woman about to have a child?"

"Not a secret, Daddy. I would have told you before. I
just . . ."

"I know," he said. "I understand. I'm just glad I
could share in it at the right time. Who knows—it may

drive me back into obstetrics." He gazed into her eyes, a gentle look of love on his face. "You did the right thing, Crista. I'm proud of you for it. You were part of something we'll cherish for the rest of our lives."

"I know," she said, looking away, feeling a warm glow come over her heart.

Suddenly he grabbed her and pulled her to his chest. "I love you, Crista."

"I love you too, Daddy."

They leaned against one another, his arm over her shoulders. The soft cries of the babies drifted out at them from the back room. "They're in for a tough time," Crista's father said. "But I think they can handle it."

"So do I," Crista answered.

·24·

Final Gift

Christmas would come in three days. The Semms settled into the guest room using two large boxes as beds for the babies. Nadine rested and Crista watched the babies nurse and even changed their tiny white diapers when Nadine was too exhausted to think.

Despite the snow, Dr. Mayfield took Johnny and Crista into town to finish up their shopping. Nadine and Johnny talked in the evening to Dr. Mayfield about Nadine's problem with doctors and he spent several hours helping her understand that even doctors make mistakes.

From the start, Dr. Mayfield allowed the two dogs into the house. At night they slept in the basement. Waiting it out, Crista geared up to ask him about keeping them, but she wasn't sure when to spring the question. She waited for the right moment, hoping he would say yes with all the other excitement.

Two days before Christmas, Crista discovered her watch was missing. She asked Nadine and Johnny about it, but they hadn't seen it. Crista worried that in the confusion of the last few days she had lost it. She hoped she would find it around the house, but it didn't appear. She worried about asking her father, for fear that he would be upset.

Christmas Day finally came. After sharing presents with Johnny and Nadine (Crista gave them the painting of Nadine from the library and some baby clothing), Dr. Mayfield gave Crista a number of presents, including art supplies, enough paper to last her the rest of the century, and a whole new set of acrylic paints. Then he produced the watch.

Crista took it with a sigh of relief. "I thought it was lost."

Her father smiled. "I sneaked it off your dresser that afternoon you fell asleep after the babies were born."

Crista stared at it, wondering what he might have done. It appeared the same.

"Turn it over," he said. "I should have had it engraved before, but maybe . . . Well, let's just say I was not thinking real clearly."

She flipped it onto its back. On the golden flat part above the "Waterproof" mark were the words, "You're God's gift to me. I love you, Dad."

Crista gave him a long hug and a kiss. He looked a bit embarrassed in front of Johnny and Nadine, but they both grinned enthusiastically. Crista wouldn't stop talking about it, even as she and Nadine got the dinner onto the table, with help from Johnny. The two babies made happy gurgling sounds in the boxes in front of the crackling fire.

Then they all sat down to a big turkey dinner. They talked about babies into the evening, and Crista even brought out the album and showed Johnny and Nadine pictures of her mother. Dr. Mayfield told several stories about how he and Crista's mother had met, but it was obvious he still felt uncomfortable about it. Crista prayed that God would give them both a peace about it.

Then after dinner, both Johnny and Dr. Mayfield ended up snoozing in chairs in the living room. Rontu and Tigger lay on the rug in front of the fire, breathing in unison and snoring happily.

Crista and Nadine cleared off the table, then sat by the picture window, each holding a baby.

"Thanks for naming the girl after me," Crista said. "It's a real honor."

"It was the obvious choice," Nadine said. "And I couldn't name her Nadine, Junior."

Both girls laughed. Little Johnny Junior in Crista's arms moved his lips and worked at opening his two blue eyes. Crista brushed at his short, dark hair.

"He really will look like Johnny," she said.

Nadine smiled. "I hope so." She peered out the window at the lake. "You have a tremendous view here."

"Someday I'd like to paint it," Crista answered, sighing happily. "Right from the table."

Nadine turned to her. "So what did he say?"

"About what?"

Crista knew what she referred to. She couldn't keep back the huge smile. "He said we could keep them—so long as I take care of them, and they sleep in the basement. But I have to get them shots and everything." She looked over at the two dogs. Tigger lay on her father's feet, warming them. The doctor's hand rested on Rontu's haunch.

Nadine squealed with delight. "I knew he'd let you!"

Crista blinked back the tears. "He said something else, too."

"Oh?" Nadine arched her eyebrows.

"He might become a baby doctor again."

Nadine whistled. "He's a good one."

"Yeah, and next time, you're going to him from the start!"

Both girls laughed.

Nadine looked across at Crista, her green eyes bright with love and admiration. "I'll always see you as my little sister."

A lump came into Crista's throat. "You're the best friend I ever had."

Nadine smiled and looked over at the two snoring men. "They look like two contented pigs, don't they?"

Crista laughed. "Yeah, but they're happy."

"So am I," Nadine said.

Catching Nadine's eye, Crista said, "I've never been happier."

They watched the babies, peered out at the lake piled high with snow, listened to the men snoring. It was a good feeling, Crista thought. Happiness. Real happiness. Somehow she knew that things with her father were changed for the better, perhaps forever. And maybe he really would become a baby doctor again. She hoped he would. He was good, and the people around the lake needed a good one.

Somehow, though, she knew it didn't matter. Whatever he did about doctoring, she knew he loved her. That was all she needed. The happiness inside her felt like a glowing piece of gold fixed deep and secure in the center of her heart.

The Action Never Stops in
The Crista Chronicles
by Mark Littleton

Secrets of Moonlight Mountain

When an unexpected blizzard traps Crista on Moonlight Mountain with a young couple in need of a doctor, Crista must brave the storm and the dark to get her physician father. Will she make it in time?

Winter Thunder

A sudden change in Crista's new friend, Jeff, and the odd circumstances surrounding Mrs. Oldham's broken windows all point to Jeff as the culprit in the recent cabin break-ins. What is Jeff trying to hide? Will Crista be able to prove his innocence?

Robbers on Rock Road

When the clues fall into place regarding the true identity of the cabin-wreckers, Crista and her friends find themselves facing terrible danger! Can they stop the robbers on Rock Road before someone gets hurt?

Escape of the Grizzly

A grizzly is on the loose on Moonlight Mountain! Who will find the bear first—the sheriff's posse or the circus workers? Crista knows there isn't much time—bear has to be found quickly. But where, and how? Doing some fast thinking, Crista has a plan...

Danger on Midnight Trail

Crista can't stand Sarah, who does everything better than Crista. But an overnight hike into the mountains, turns into a nightmare for Crista and Sarah. Can Crista and Sarah put aside their differences to save Crista's dad and face the danger on Midnight Trail?

Up-Beat.
Up-Tempo. Up-Lifting.

And you don't have to go to
Upper Mongolia to find them. Because author Mark
Littleton is up to good things,
and he's written a fantastic devotional series for teens
that's up for grabs at your local Christian bookstore.
Each book is designed to give
your spiritual life the powerful pick up it needs.
With four up-to-date titles to choose from, you're
bound to pick a winner.

BEEFIN' UP: *Daily Feed for Amazing Grazing*
TUNIN' UP: *Daily Jammin' for Tight Relationships*
FILLIN' UP: *Daily Fuel for High Performance Living*
PAIRIN' UP: *The Ultimate Dating and Relating Guide for Teens*

The choice is up to you.

MULTNOMAH BOOKS

Don't Miss Any of the
Addie McCormick Adventures!
by Leanne Lucas

The Stranger in the Attic

A vanishing visitor and secrets from the past... Can Addie and Nick put the puzzle together before something terrible happens to their friend Miss T.?

The Mystery of the Missing Scrapbook

A missing scrapbook, mysterious paintings, and an old letter lead Nick, Addie, and Brian on a heartstopping chase. Are they in over their heads this time?

The Stolen Statue

A movie star has been kidnapped and Miss T.'s statue has disappeared! Addie has all the clues... but can she put them together before it's too late?

The Chicago Surprise

When Addie and Nick catch a thief, what they discover about the culprit is much more than they bargained for!

The Mystery of the Skeleton Key

In Addie's family history, there's a "treasure" that no one can find! Will Addie be able to solve a mystery that's more than 100 years old?

The Computer Pirate

Someone is stealing information from the school's computer system! Addie's friend is the #1 suspect. Can she prove his innocence?

The Secret of the Scarlet Box

Addie and Nick find an old lockbox with clues for a special treasure hunt planned by a man 50 years ago! Can they find the last clue and the treasure before anyone else?

Capturing the Spirit
of the Next Generation...

The Class of 2000
by Ginny Williams

Second Chances

At 15 years old, Kelly finds her life in sudden turmoil when her widowed father decides to remarry. Struggling with bitter feelings, Kelly determines that she'll never accept her father's wife. But a beautiful black horse, a special friend, and a daring rescue from a burning barn give Kelly a different perspective on those she loves...and a chance to start over with her new stepmother.

A Matter of Trust

God changed Kelly's heart, but now she's finding it difficult sometimes for her actions to follow. Conflict at home threatens to tear the family apart. But when her beloved horse almost dies, Kelly discovers strength and support from an unlikely source—her stepmom.

Lost-and-Found Friend

Kelly's friend Brent is a very sensitive, very intense person who is adept at hiding his troubles. When pressures at home become overwhelming, Brent attempts suicide. Concerned friends, a ski trip, and a life-threatening snowstorm help Brent realize there are alternative ways to solve his problems.